THE SHEPHERD'S SON AND THE LADY

A VICTORIAN CHRISTMAS MIRACLE

DOLLY PRICE

PUREREAD.COM

Copyright © 2023 PureRead Ltd

www.pureread.com

All rights reserved. No part of this publication may be reproduced, distributed or transmitted in any form or by any means, without prior written permission.

Publisher's Note: This is a work of fiction. Names, characters, places, and incidents are a product of the author's imagination. Locales and public names are sometimes used for atmospheric purposes. Any resemblance to actual people, living or dead, or to businesses, companies, events, institutions, or locales is completely coincidental.

CONTENTS

Dear reader, get ready for another great story… 1
1. HETHERTON 3
2. THE DALTONS 7
3. SHEPHERDS ON THE HILLS 10
4. PLANS FOR CALEB 14
5. THE APPRENTICE 18
6. THE GRANVILLE CONNECTION 23
7. UP IN THE WORLD 26
8. CALEB HOME 31
9. KEEPING UP APPEARANCES 35
10. CHRISTMAS AT WHITHOLM 39
11. AUNT KITTY FINDS LOVE 43
12. ALICE'S PARASOL 47
13. LAVISH—AND FOOLISH 50
14. CHRISTMAS POVERTY 53
15. CHRISTMAS CONSOLATIONS 58
16. FROM BAD TO WORSE 63
17. VANISHED 67
18. HENRY'S PLAN 70
19. LIVING AT WHITHOLM 77
20. UNHAPPINESS 81
21. BABS TAKES CHARGE 83
22. AN UNHOLY CHRISTMAS 87
23. TO LONDON 92
24. THE QUARREL 95
25. BROWNTON WORKHOUSE 99
26. ESCAPE 103
27. THE LAUNDRY 106
28. STREET SINGER 110
29. DARK DECEMBER 114
30. CRISIS ON CHRISTMAS EVE 118
31. THE RESCUER 121

32.	ST BARTHOLOMEW'S	126
33.	DALTON'S CHRISTMAS	130
34.	RECOVERING	136
35.	A NEW BEGINNING	139
36.	HARVEY VERNON	143
37.	AN OLD SHEPHERD'S ADVICE	147
38.	PIP'S TROUBLE	150
39.	BABS IN SERVICE	154
40.	THE WORST NEWS	159
41.	BABS'S DAYDREAMS	164
42.	THE MEETING	168
43.	RETURN TO SWANNS FURNITURE	171
44.	CHRISTMAS HEARTBREAK	176
45.	MRS. DEBORAH DELAMERE	179
46.	LETTER TO CALEB	183
47.	PIP AND ALICE	187
48.	ANOTHER RETURN	193
49.	THE ROSEWOOD TABLE	197
50.	MISS SWANN VISITS	200
51.	A GIANT YELLOW LAMPSHADE	203
52.	CHIPPY ON HER MIND	209
53.	CALEB IS THANKED	213
54.	STELLA NAMES THE DAY	217
55.	MR. SWANN'S ILLNESS	220
56.	MOURNING	224
57.	THE MASTERPIECE	228
58.	VERNON'S REVENGE!	234
59.	RECOVERY	237
60.	THE REVELATION	247
61.	RETURN TO HETHERTON	254
	Love Victorian Christmas Saga Romance?	271
	Have You Read?	276
	Our Gift To You	287

DEAR READER, GET READY FOR ANOTHER GREAT STORY...

A VICTORIAN ROMANCE

Turn the page and let's begin

HETHERTON

The village of Hetherton was tucked away in a valley ten miles north of Chelmsford in Essex. In former days its few humble and unassuming streets were more deserving of the term hamlet, though there was a baker, a butcher, a school and a church (with a low spire) interspersed with rows of small stone thatched cottages in which lived a blacksmith, a farrier, and a carpenter who was also the undertaker. All made a fair living, with the undertaker whose nickname was 'Coff' Willis, the richest of all. Then the railway came, and a station was built. The population of Hetherton increased, as now it was possible for people to work in the City and live in the country, and a few new, good-sized houses were built on one hillside, and the village as a consequence grew in population and importance. Soon there were two of everything—butchers, bakers, chandlers, blacksmiths and even an emporium, which sold everything from brooms to kid gloves.

Most of the land was owned by a gentleman named Withers, who welcomed the new gentry as an addition to society. His was a large home overlooking everybody else's, his home farm was large and he was the main employer in the district surrounding the village. An ancestor of his had come from Dorset, but missed his sheep, so he had sent for his large flocks and the shepherds, one of whom was a Dalton, who drove them all the way from Dorset to Essex.

Farms surrounded Hetherton. Farm labourers and shepherds lived in cottages either in the village or on the hillsides. If they ever went to London, (and a few of them risked it) it was to return again and complain about the noise, the hurry and the stinking river and how they would never go again.

Mr. Wren was one of those men whose occupations lay in the City, but who built a house in Hetherton after the train service began. He called his house Redgate because it stood on Redgate Hill, and settled in when his family was young. His eldest son Henry was some years older than the other three and was a favourite of his mother, as he had all her attention for a full eight years before the second child. The three youngest children were born closer in age, with only a year between Pip and Babs. They grew up as creatures of the fields almost as much as the cottagers' children, loving to be out-of-doors, whereas Henry disdained company that was below theirs.

The youngest, Barbara, was a great favourite of her father and in her later years would tell her grandchildren of how the family used to spend Christmas Night, for that memory stood out for her more than any other and belonged to a time before 'the great trouble and London,' which came later. The memory of those Christmasses sustained her in the hardest times.

Christmas Eve was a time of fevered preparation and, for the children, anticipation of the morrow. But no presents were to be opened before the visit to the church for the early service, and the excitement was almost too much to bear on the carriage ride home. Then their Christmas stockings were taken down and out tumbled toys and sweets, and there was a great clamour while Mrs. Curtin, the cook, prepared a hot breakfast. In the late morning, the children went out for a long walk with their dogs Rex and Caesar and returned when Christmas dinner was ready.

Every Christmas night they gathered in the cosy parlour around a blazing fire to sing carols. All were tired by then, and very happy. The dinner in the afternoon had ended only as dusk approached, and they went to church again in the evening, and returned to eat cold ham and Christmas cake. The adults drank coffee; the children, cocoa. They then went to the candlelit parlour. The children were allowed to eat bonbons and gingerbread, which their mother would never allow in that room at any other time.

Aunt Kitty, who lived with them, sat at the piano and led a carol service. Babs sat on her father's lap, trying to stay awake, listening to the joyful sounds and the crackling of the fire. Everybody had a turn singing, and before she was able to sing properly her father helped her to sing 'The First Nowell,' in his low crooning voice. The fire was not allowed to go down, and they stayed up late.

THE DALTONS

Babs knew that shepherds looked after the sheep, and she knew that the Dalton family on the side of Hetherton Hill were shepherds. She and her brothers were playmates of the children there. The roof was thatch, with no ceiling, and occasionally an insect tumbled from the bound straw onto the head or shoulders of someone inside. There was a vegetable garden behind the house and a pig was kept in a shed along with a donkey and their winter supply of fuel, mostly peat and sticks and twigs, for coal was expensive.

They had a large fireplace in the main room. The house at Redgate had a range for cooking and baking, but Mrs. Dalton had pots and pans that she attached to hooks to cook on the open fire. She baked barley bread on the fire. Her husband took the bread out into the fields with him for his lunch, along with a slice of bacon or a hunk of cheese. 'Sheppy Alf' as he was locally known went out every morning, rain or shine, dressed in a knee-length shirt called a smock-frock, a warm cloak, leggings and boots, with his dog by his side and his shepherd's crook.

Bets loved watching Mrs. Dalton bake bread. She did not have such an interesting spectacle at home. The cook shooed her out of the kitchen whenever she appeared there, and her mother scolded her for 'bothering Cook and making her forget what she was doing.'

Mrs. Wren tended to scold a great deal. She had worries. Her greatest worry was that she was not good enough for the gentry, for she was the daughter of a tradesman. She spent a great deal of money and energy outfitting her children, her table, and her house to appear better than she felt it was.

Mr. Wren worked hard at his import business in the City. The village of Hetherton was not very far from the centre of business in London and he travelled there by train. His partner in business was a Mr. Burlington who was gifted in financial matters, while Mr. Wren supplied the charm and sociability to attract and keep customers. He often stayed over at his club in order to entertain them. Babs was always disappointed if her father was not at home in the evenings. She adored her Papa.

Aunt Kitty was her father's sister, and Babs could not remember a time when she did not live with them, though she knew that a long time ago, she had lived with her widowed mother and brother, both of whom had died.

She was not married. Debts had been discovered after her brother's death and the settling of these obligations had left her without the means to sustain herself.

Aunt Kitty resigned herself to spending her life as the poor relation and made herself useful to her sister-in-law as much as she could. Aunt Kitty saw that Gladys Wren had little patience with her children, so she undertook the care of them, while Mrs. Wren was free to plan improvements for the house. The Withers lived in a manor house in a spacious park, and whenever Mrs. Withers paid a call she felt the inadequacy of her own home, and wondered if Mrs. Withers thought about her inferior furnishings all the way home in her carriage.

SHEPHERDS ON THE HILLS

As Babs grew, Aunt Kitty taught her about Jesus and read Bible stories to her.

"Now there's King David, he was tending the sheep when the prophet Samuel asked to see him."

"A King out on the hills tending the sheep!"

"Oh, he was not King yet—that was later. But just think, Babs, how great God's plans are for us!"

"The Daltons are shepherds," Babs said, as her admiration for her playmates grew. "But Auntie, when Jesus was born why did the angels appear first to shepherds? Why didn't they go to—to the Mayor of Bethlehem—or somebody rich?"

"Because, dear Babs, God does not see us the way we see each other. God does not think that people with money and nice china and furniture and bigger houses are worth more than people who do not have those things."

Babs was silent and wondered about this for a long time.

"My, you are a ponderer!" Aunt Kitty chuckled at her faraway look. "What are you thinking, child?"

"That if Jesus was born here in Hetherton, the Heavenly Host would have appeared to the Daltons or the Tarrants and they would have been the first to see Him! And visit him! Not the Withers! Not us!"

"That is fine indeed, and very true, but now it's time to stop dreaming and to practise your piano, for there is only a half-hour left before dinner," Aunt Kitty said.

These heavenly thoughts elevated the Daltons in Babs's eyes. When she and Pip had a holiday from lessons they went to the fields where the sheep were being pastured. Caleb was often there with his father. They watched the sheepdog expertly follow commands. When they gave Ranger commands, he took no notice at all.

"Have you been to the sheep again?" their mother asked them one day. "It's not fitting that you spend so much time with the shepherds."

"But Mama, Mr. Withers comes by often, and Master Robert and Miss Margaret also, and they play with us," Pip rejoined.

"Were they there today?" Mrs Wren asked doubtfully.

"Yes, Mama, they were there." Babs said. "But Mama, do you know that Ranger won't take orders from Mr. Withers? He tried it and Ranger just looked at him and did nothing! Isn't that funny? Mr. Withers mustn't be so important after all!"

"Ranger only has one master, and that's Sheppy Alf," Pip said.

The Withers children only turned up sporadically with their father. After that summer, they hardly went at all. Master Robert was sent away to school and Miss Margaret had a strict governess. They met at church on Sundays. It puzzled Babs why the rich people of the district went up to the front, and the tradesmen and their families and poor people were always behind them at the back. If God saw no difference, why did the vicar?

Her mother tried to foster a friendship between Miss Margaret and Babs and was affronted when there was no interest on the Withers side. Miss Margaret was three years older than Babs in any case, so she dropped it.

Babs was content with the friends she had, Alice Dalton and her brother Caleb, who was not to go away to school. There was Betsy Tarrant and other girls who were happy to play with her.

Every Christmas Eve on her way upstairs with her candle, Babs paused and looked out on the darkened hillside where a pinpoint of light and smoke from the chimney marked the Dalton cottage, and in her mind's eye the deep blue sky vanished, and was filled with angels bathed in heavenly light and singing joyful praises to God. She lingered there and pondered until Aunt Kitty called from her room to ask her why she was delayed.

PLANS FOR CALEB

The younger Wren children knew almost as much about sheep and lambs as the Dalton children. They knew the individuals of the flock almost as intimately as their playmates. There were one or two strong personalities among them that caused them amusement. They loved Ranger as much as they loved their own dogs. Babs and Alice fed the orphaned lambs with care and tenderness. The shepherd's children also roved the grounds of Redgate House, played on the see-saw and swung from the big oak, and ate apples when they were ripe.

Babs was petite for her age, with creamy skin, dark hair and large dark eyes. She was lively and could climb a tree almost as high as her brother Pip. Her friend Alice had sandy-coloured hair and green eyes and freckles. She was taller than Babs and filled with life and energy.

Caleb, like his sister, had sandy hair and green eyes. He was tall like his father Alf, and he was several years the girls' and Pip's senior but joined in their games between his many chores and duties. He spent his days with the sheep whittling wood into useful objects and toys. He was a gifted craftsman and could make anything with his hands. He fashioned a skipping rope with elaborate handles on each end for his sister Alice and painted it in her favourite colours. He made Pip a whistle which had such a piercing sound he was not allowed to use it in the house.

He also made a mouth organ. He took an old one to pieces to find out how it worked and made a new one from pieces of scrap metal from the blacksmiths and walnut for the casing, into which he put a seashell inlay, and polished with rosin begged from Coff Willis. He was very proud of it, and gave it to Alice, who gave it to Babs in exchange for a straw bonnet. He did not mind, for Babs appreciated it, and Alice was not interested in music.

Every summer the village had dances on the green. There were morris dances performed by the older boys in the village. They wore smock-frocks banded with colourful sashes and tied as many sheep's-bells as would fit to their leggings, painted their faces and danced to the music of Old Mo's accordion. They formed patterns and figures of eight and the noisy jangling of the bells added to the very entertaining spectacle for the village. Caleb was a favourite performer, as his father had been in his day, as his height allowed him to leap higher than every other lad, for leaping was a great part of it. The women also performed their dances wearing clogs and carrying hoops adorned with bright ribbons, forming intricate patterns as they danced. Alice and Babs were too young to join in but loved watching them and practiced it on their own as part of their games.

Sheppy Alf had had no schooling, but Caleb went to the local national school. He was a quick learner and this gave his mother a great deal to think about, for the shepherd's life is a hard, lonely one, out in all weathers, and she thought he would do better with a trade.

"It seems such a pity to take him out," Mrs. Dalton had said to her husband when Caleb was only ten years old. "He's so gifted with 'is hands that if 'e had a bit more education, he could become apprenticed to a Cabinet Maker. There was a Swan family in Colchester not far from where I was in service, and they now have a place in London and are said to be doing very well. Oh I know you need the 'elp, Alf, but Alice can 'elp you more. She's every bit as good with the sheep as Caleb."

"She won't be able to help you in the house 'n, Dolly." Alf remarked. "You'll 'ave to do all the spinnin' as well as everything else."

Dorothy Dalton had a spinning wheel. It was a time-consuming task and there was less demand for homespun cloth now than before, what with all the cotton factories in the towns and cities. But Dolly had a little market among the villagers for her skeins of yarn which she dyed herself. Knitting was becoming popular, though the upper classes disdained it as yet.

"I'll make the sacrifice for Caleb," was the reply.

And the parents saved as much as they could to keep their boy in school and to save for the apprenticeship fee. He helped also, because there was a demand for wooden household items, from spoons to coffins. The former he made at home in his spare time; with the latter he assisted Coff Willis. Everybody for miles around knew how gifted Caleb Dalton was with his hands and he was called 'Chippy Dalton' from a young age. He could make anything. The schoolmaster Mr. Coolidge made enquiries to Swanns Furniture and discovered that Mr. Swann would not take any boy who did not have at least eight years of schooling. They turned most away.

Mr. Coolidge encouraged Caleb, and he it was who found out the particular skills that Mr. Swann desired in an apprentice. He made Caleb put down his designs on paper, and took him to London himself to see the great man who was making a name for himself among the rich and fashionable of the City, for Sheppy Alf did not like London and was not equal to a mission of this sort. He knew that the schoolmaster would be a better advocate for his son.

THE APPRENTICE

Babs and Pip Wren ran down the hill one day to play with their friends to find that Caleb was sitting in the cottage, scrubbed clean with his Sunday suit and cap on, and a pair of boots on his feet.

"Where are you going?" they chorused.

"He's going to Town," Alice explained. "Look, he has a box full of the things he made to show Mr. Swann."

"Who is Mr. Swann?" asked Pip.

"He's very important and makes furniture. Caleb is going to be apprenticed to him. He has to show him what he can do, so that's why he has to bring the box."

The Wren children lost no time examining the box containing drawings, wooden animals and birds, whistles, and small useful items when the Master came bustling in, saying that he had been delayed and would miss the train if they didn't hurry. The box was hastily fastened, and they set out.

"Caleb!" Babs called after him. She pulled the mouth organ from her pinafore pocket. "Take this too! Show him this!"

Caleb slipped it into his pocket and he and Mr. Coolidge walked on, out of sight.

After a ride in the train and a walk through a maze of streets, schoolmaster and boy came to Whitechapel, to a large building in Ferry Street which housed Mr. Swann's shop, his factory, and to the right, his gracious house. His showrooms were in front, and the workshop spread out toward the back, towards a boneyard. Caleb's eyes grew round with wonder at the impressive building he hoped to learn his trade. They were shown into a small office and waited. After some minutes a working man in a long apron came in and shut the door.

"How can I 'elp you?" he asked.

"We are waiting to see Mr. Swann," said Mr. Coolidge.

"Tha's me. I'm in a hurry, so if you would state your business without delay, I'd be grateful."

He not only looked like a working man, he spoke like one, with a broad country accent.

"This boy wishes to become your apprentice," Mr. Coolidge said, his hand on Caleb's shoulder.

Mr. Swann signalled for the materials they were holding and without bidding them to be seated, he opened the box which held the boy's drawings and samples of his work. Caleb was nervous, but he smelled the sawdust and heard the sound of saws somewhere about, so he was excited too. What were they making in the factory?

It did not seem hopeful at first. As Mr. Swann picked up each drawing and sample, he frowned, raised his eyebrows, narrowed his eyes, grunted, and set them aside.

"Is that all?" he asked, and both hearts sank. "We demand a very 'igh standard of talent and workmanship. What 'ave you got there, me lad?" he asked as Caleb hastily drew an object from his pocket.

"It's a mouth organ, sir."

"Give it 'ere,"

"Did you make this?" he asked, turning it over in his hand.

"Yes, sir."

"And did you put this inlay in?"

"Yes, sir."

"What did you use to cut it to shape?"

"Just a wooden saw, sir."

"And what else? What's the inlay made of?"

"It's a seashell, sir, that I was given."

"And what did you polish the casing with?"

"Turpentine and resin from the undertaker, sir, I 'elp him make coffins."

"And would you be prepared to come and live in London? Here with my family, with the other apprentices in the servants' wing, knowing your place?"

"Yes, sir," Caleb said.

"Behaving properly, never give any trouble? Working 'ard, long hours? For seven years?"

"I'll work hard and never be any trouble, sir!" Caleb promised, hardly daring to believe that this was happening to him. Mr. Coolidge's mood had gone from dejection to elation, and he vouched warmly for Caleb and for the character of his family.

"The premium is ten pounds," Mr. Swann addressed the schoolmaster.

"That much! His parents are shepherds, not living on more than fifty a year, I would think."

"Tell them it will be worth it, however it can be managed. He will get a great training 'ere and then he can do as he pleases, naming 'is price."

"Sir, is that ten pounds every year?" Caleb knew that if the answer was yes, it was hopeless.

Mr. Swann looked at him with a paternal expression.

"No, me lad, it's just once, a sort of insurance to make you stay out the first few years when your work will be boring, for you start at the bottom. For the first year you'll be sweeping, running errands, cleanin' machinery and makin' glue from boiled-down bones. You won't be makin' furniture for a while. For the last four years of your apprenticeship, if you stay that long, I will pay you a wage. Of course, on your own time, you can make what you like from leftover raw material. Don't forget your mouth organ."

"Thank you, sir." Caleb was immensely relieved.

Caleb departed his home village for London when he was fourteen years old.

He left a void after him in Hetherton. His mother and father missed him acutely, his sister cried, and Bets and Pip were very disappointed that he would hardly to be seen in Hetherton from now on, only at Christmas and for a short holiday in the summer. But life went on. Babs continued to be tutored by Aunt Kitty, Henry and Geoff went back to school (a good school, the same as the Withers boy!) and Pip was to begin this term.

Babs would be on her own except for Alice, who she did not see very much of now, unless she helped her with her many chores looking after the animals.

THE GRANVILLE CONNECTION

The fact that her sons were at the same public school as the Withers boy meant extra worries for Mrs Wren. For they had to have the same quality linens and clothes and sporting equipment and had to be sent a generous allowance, for to be seen as poor was an unbearable state of things. Henry alone appreciated this and constantly asked for more. Henry shared her love of status and rank, and worked to cultivate upper class ways, imitating his better peers at school, careful never to allow them to know his father was not Old Money.

Henry made a friend of a boy named Frederick Granville who had a sister, Irene. They came from Whitholm, about ten miles from Hetherton. She and her parents visited Freddie frequently and Henry was often of the party when they went out on carriage drives and picnics, and he spent several holidays with them, and became almost as familiar with the Granville manor house and estate as he was with his own home.

To Mrs. Wren's great wonder, Miss Irene Granville fell in love with her son Henry. Her next thought brought the fear of social humiliation.

"The Granvilles will oppose the match and show us up as poor," she lamented to her husband.

"And is that all you care about?" he asked. "Good grief, Mrs. Wren, your son's heart is about to be broken and you only care that he will show us up!"

"Oh, Henry is not in love with Miss Granville. He only thinks he is."

Mrs. Wren was not wrong in her assessment. Miss Granville was not beautiful, or vivacious, she did not flirt, she had gathered no crowd of admirers about her. Had she no fortune, Henry would never have thought any romantic thoughts about her. But as it dawned upon him that she was singling him out for attention, that she looked his way, that she slipped her arm into his at every opportunity, it also dawned upon him that he might be wealthy in the future. Henry was not a passionate man. Only the thought of luxury and ease excited him.

Indeed, I could be very happy with her, he said to himself. *She does not irritate me like many young ladies, her manner is easy and her temper quiet, and she has a great deal of money—what more needs to be said? I would be a fool to turn away.*

He returned her affection with all the passion his lazy nature could muster, and he now had to get up the courage to ask her father for her hand in marriage. He invented prospects; rich uncles; anything would do to get this girl to the altar, but Mr. Granville cut him short.

"If my daughter wants to marry you, I will not stand in her way," he said before he had a chance to mention the mythical uncle. "As it happens, I am tired of running our large estate; so this could be very timely indeed. Frederick, you know, is destined for the Bar. He has his heart set on it. But you, my son-to-be, shall take his place here. You shall live here, and I shall pay you a salary. You will not inherit it of course, that is my son's birthright, but I hope that by the time I go to my rest that you will have compiled a goodly sum for yourself and for my daughter, for her ten thousand pounds will not last forever, and there will be a clause in the marriage contract that you must consult her before you spend more than one hundred pounds."

Henry swallowed. Work! No financial independence unless he worked! He was almost tempted to withdraw his proposal, but had not the courage to do so, and he would go ahead with it and make the best of things.

UP IN THE WORLD

The happy news spread, the wedding was fixed for New Year's Day, and Mrs. Granville called upon Mrs. Wren at the first opportunity. She did not send word beforehand, and Mrs. Wren looked out the window and saw what must be Mrs. Granville's carriage approach her front door, for it was exactly as Henry described. The usual worries surged to her head—was the house clean? Warm enough for her Ladyship? What a shame the silver was being polished at that very moment—they would have to use the Wedgewood for tea. They now had a standard to keep up. She sent upstairs for Kitty, for she found it tiresome to make conversation and Kitty was chatty. Her sister-in-law came down and brought Babs with her, and she sat quietly while the ladies chatted about wedding plans. Mrs. Granville had come to invite the family over to Whitholm House on Christmas Day for their dinner, and to stay the night!

"We would be honoured to, Mrs. Granville!" said Mrs Wren.

"We have family members coming for the wedding, and we thought they might come for Christmas, so as to make a good holiday out of it. It will be nice for you all to meet and to get to know each other before the wedding day, which I think is always so busy one never gets to talk to anybody properly."

"We would be so happy to attend you on Christmas Day," gushed Mrs. Wren. She then began to worry about what everybody was to wear. Not the same gowns as the wedding, of course! It was double trouble, but she could not refuse.

Babs could not understand why anybody would want to marry her brother Henry. He was grumpy and cross. He never paid her any attention except to tell her to go away. Miss Granville must be very silly to like him!

The wedding was to be a few days after Christmas, and she cheered up. She loved Christmas! Now after it was over, instead of being sad that it would be a long time before next Christmas, she could look forward to the wedding.

As the day approached, she began to wish that Henry was not getting married. For her mother was in a fever of nerves about it all. Babs escaped when she could to the Dalton cottage to see Alice and to help her feed the animals and bring in sticks for the fire. She it was who brought the news to the Wren family that Caleb was expected home on Christmas Eve for two full weeks!

But her news, instead of bringing interest to her mother, brought an unpleasant command on the day before Christmas Eve.

"You and Pip are not to go to the Dalton cottage again. They are not to come here. You are not to play with those children any longer."

Mrs. Wren immediately began to think of something else and left the room, but Babs followed her.

"Why, Mama, why can't we see the Daltons again?"

"Why? You shouldn't have to ask me why, Babs, you're not a small child anymore. Can you not see the difference between them and us?"

"But you never minded before!"

"Before was a different time. Now we are to be very well-connected and have to be more prudent in choosing our friendships. I will send down a jelly on Christmas Eve, and Hetty will take it, not you and Pip. When Alice is older she may be in service here as a kitchen maid, and you can see how odd it would be for you to have been her friend. Hetty, do you have the lace on the petticoat yet?"

Her mother had entered the work room where the maids were feverishly sewing. Babs followed, determined to speak more.

"Mama!"

"What is it, Babs?"

"The shepherds were the first people to see Baby Jesus!"

"Well, I know that, why do you speak of it?"

"Because the Daltons are shepherds!"

Her mother caught her by the arm and pulled her into the hallway.

"You are the most impertinent child I ever met in my life. It's as well to break off this friendship now, indeed it should have been done a long time ago! You have learned your boldness from them. Go to your room and stay there for the rest of the day; you are in disgrace."

Babs began to weep and ran to her room. Aunt Kitty was on the way in from an errand, she heard the commotion and sought her sister-in-law to enquire what had happened. She met her in the hallway. She was unprepared for the attack upon her.

"It's you—Kitty—you put ideas into her head. I do not know why the shepherds were the first people to see Our Lord Jesus, but to try to say that the Daltons are deserving of any notice because of that is ridiculous. They are low-class people and they're not fit company for us. I have forbidden the children to see them anymore. I wish you had forbidden it, for I have entrusted my daughter to your care, and now I shall have no confidence in you. I would prefer if you do not seek out Barbara now in the mistaken belief that she needs comfort. She has been very, very impertinent."

Kitty stood in the hall, humiliated. She had felt that as long as she was a good teacher of Babs, that her role in the house and in the family was valued. But to be reprimanded thus! She wished she could pack her things and leave the house, but she had nowhere to go. She could hear Babs weeping in her room.

On Christmas Eve as night fell, Babs looked out of her window. She had heard the train come to the station and seen the puff of smoke as it left again. She strained her eyes in the gathering dusk when she saw a long-legged youth with a pack on his back go through the village. It was Caleb! She longed to open the window and call out to him but dared not. He would not hear her anyway. She watched him all the way home until he turned to go up Hetherton Hill, then the cottage swallowed him up.

CALEB HOME

As Caleb entered the cottage there was a joyful chorus as the family, Ranger included, rushed to welcome him. He beamed from ear to ear at the beloved faces and the cheery fire and the smell of mince pies. They crowded him about and spoke all at once —how was the City? How long could he stay? What was Mr Swann like? Were his quarters nice? Why did he not write more often? This last came from his mother, who could not read. Pip Wren or Alice read out his letters to her and to Alf and she kept them all in a little oaken box that Caleb had fashioned for her treasures. He rubbed the happy dog's head as he related his news to them.

"It's like a different country, this is," he said. "When I first went to London, I didn't think I could bide there, with the people 'urrying past me, and nobody looking my way at all, and if I nodded a greeting they were startled as wild rabbits, and then there was the bad air, the soot going into my lungs, the stink from the river, but the thought of you losing the ten pounds kept me at it. Tonight, when I got off the train, I got such air into my lungs, I didn't mind the cold of it, it was that fresh."

In London he shared a room with the other two apprentices, and it was all right, they were good lads, though from London and couldn't understand him nor he them. Every Sunday the apprentices ate their dinner with the family. The Swanns were a nice family and not ones to act superior. Mr. Swann had been an apprentice and had no airs. They were rich now, his quality furniture was known everywhere, and Caleb was proud to belong to the house and to the business, for to be trained under Mr. Swann would give him distinction in his trade, though he wouldn't settle in London, oh no, he'd come back to Hetherton and set up a furniture factory.

Caleb had gained a mature air befitting a contented youth but was not in any way high and mighty after his season in the City. After he had been placed at the table and plied with mince pies, he asked for the Wrens.

"Oh all excitement up at the 'ouse!" Alice exclaimed. "Henry is to marry a very rich girl! They haven't come down today, Mama. Pip and Babs, tha' is. Shouldn't they have come to visit by now?"

A short time later a knock came to the door, and Alice rushed to open it. But it was the parlourmaid, Hetty, clad in a cloak and hood who stood there with a dish covered by a cloth in her hands.

"It's good to see you, Hetty," Mrs. Dalton said, ushering her in. "Ah I see you have got our trifle there! Mrs. Wren is so generous to send us a trifle every Christmas! Oh—oh but it's—a jelly." Dolly's voice fell as Hetty uncovered the dish.

"With the compliments of my mistress, Mrs. Dalton," Hetty said. "And wishing you a Merry Christmas from all up at Redgate House."

"And to you too, and all at the 'ouse," Dolly Dalton said. Hetty took her leave and there was a deflated air in the little dwelling.

"Well that never 'appened before," Caleb remarked. "No trifle, and no Pip nor Babs!"

"Why did she not send Pip and Babs? They always came before," Alice said a little sadly. "And—why are we only getting a jelly? It's a very nice jelly to be sure, but..."

"No trifle for dessert tomorrow," Dolly said. "A jelly indeed! What is it, raspberry? And not even a bowl of custard! But we have to be thankful for what we got."

"I expect there be economies up in that 'ouse," Alf said, spitting into the fire as was his custom when smoking his pipe. "For the wedding, you know."

"The bride's father pays for the wedding, Papa," Alice pointed out.

"Since the Granvilles are richer than they be, they might be going all out with their clobber." Caleb grinned. Alice then asked about the style of the Swann ladies.

"Mrs. Swann likes black and sort of purple, I think. Miss Swann gets 'erself up nicely enough. All colours, bright-like."

"What's Miss Swann like?" Alice was eager to hear about how a young lady of the City dressed and conducted herself. But her brother was a very poor informant of young ladies of fashion and spoke instead of a young man named Harvey Vernon, who was a relation of some sort, but who Mr. Swann was at odds with.

KEEPING UP APPEARANCES

Night had fallen and no customary visit was paid by the Wren children. In the house on the hill, when Hetty brought in the tea things that evening, Mrs. Wren asked her about her visit to the cottage.

"What did Mrs. Dalton say to the gelatine?"

"She remarked it, remarked that it wasn't a trifle, Ma'am." Hetty said.

"Indeed!"

"You only sent them a jelly this year?" Henry asked. "Mama, what that says to the cottagers is that we may be counting our pennies." Henry, as he was to marry into a wealthy family, felt he knew exactly how things should be done.

"Oh, I did not mean to give that impression!" Mrs. Wren exclaimed. "As it is, we don't have to send anything at all, we do so only out of the kindness of our hearts for our poorer neighbours. The cottage belongs to the Withers, not us."

"But you have set a precedent with a trifle, Mama. The higher you are, the more you give to your less fortunate neighbours at Christmas," Henry pointed out with severity.

"Oh dear! What does Mrs. Granville give?"

"I heard Irene say that cook was very busy making little hampers of cake, sweetmeats and jams to send down to them."

"Oh dear—well—I shall know next year."

"I wouldn't like it put about that we are strapped for money," Mr. Wren put in sternly. "This will be spoken of in the village. So I propose you tell Cook to make a trifle and send it down in the morning."

"Oh dear, Cook will not like it at all. But I suppose we must, to save face. And a bowl of custard. It's a good thing we only have one cottage nearby. How many do the Granvilles have, Henry?"

"Mother, they have the village of Whitholm on their land. What do you think? A street of cottages as well as dozens of tenants scattered about their estate." Henry always sounded impatient and patronising.

"Oh, what a lot of work that is at Christmas time! But I suppose only the favoured ones get presents."

The parlourmaid found herself walking down to the Dalton cottage the following morning. She was rather cross, as Cook had been angry and made her do most of the work, though she was not supposed to work in the kitchen.

The cottagers were surprised.

"Yesterday was a mistake," Hetty repeated what she had been told to say, in a rather monotonous tone. "This was meant to be sent down. Here is a trifle and custard."

"How good of Mrs. Wren! Give her our thanks and best wishes!"

"Where are Master Pip and Miss Babs?" Alice asked.

Hetty smirked.

"They'll not come down anymore," she said meaningfully. "Now that Master Henry is marrying high. I will have to bid you good day now and a Merry Christmas."

"Snobs they be, the Wrens." Alf said after she had left, dipping his forefinger into the custard to bring a little dab to his tongue. "Oh, this tastes well. Sweet it is."

Caleb felt annoyed that the Wrens now felt they were above the Daltons, so far above that they would not visit even at Christmas time. The difference in class had never mattered much when they were children, but as they were growing up, a gap was developing.

"Shall we go to see them?" Alice asked wistfully. "I want to tell Babs 'ow Rascal goes on." Rascal was an orphaned lamb who was now almost grown. She was a great pet. "And Pip said he'd race me to the oak tree. I can run as fast as he can."

"No, we won't go," Caleb said firmly. "You 'ave to forget about Babs bein' your friend from now on. You 'ave other friends. And I've made friends in London. We don't need the Wrens, Alice. Don't grieve for 'em, it's the way of the world, it is."

CHRISTMAS AT WHITHOLM

The dining room at Whitholm House was like nothing the Wrens had ever seen. A snow-white damask tablecloth covered the long table laden with crystal bowls, candlesticks and gold and silver decorations. There were about thirty places laid and each sparkled with silver. There was a great blaze in the fireplace.

They were introduced to the greater family—a collection of cousins mostly, and a few children who were splendidly dressed and who Mrs. Wren observed to have faultless manners.

Aunt Kitty had rehearsed several carols, and Babs was looking forward to singing 'Hark the Herald Angels Sing' in the evening. Mrs. Wren knew that though money could buy many accomplishments, it could not purchase a superior singing voice, and the Wrens had uncommonly good voices. She had already ascertained that Irene Granville could not sing a note and it followed that the rest of the family had little or no musical ability, and she looked forward to her family claiming a place in the limelight in the evening entertainments.

But she and the other members of the Wren family were to be gravely disappointed. After Christmas dinner, they were ushered to the warm and spacious drawing room, where several small tables had been set out, and the grand piano closed and covered in a purple cloth.

There was to be an evening of card-playing.

"*Cards!*" Aunt Kitty said in a low tone, shocked. "On Christmas Night of all nights! Oh, what is become of us in this day and age?"

Nobody was pleased—and the children were not to stay up. The Granville children's nurse took them away, and it was obvious that the younger Wrens should go as well. Aunt Kitty hurried to usher Pip and Babs upstairs hoping this way to escape the devil's amusement.

"I don't like it here," Babs said crossly as she knelt to say her prayers. "I had my song all ready! And Pip was to sing *Good King Wenceslas*."

Kitty stayed up there for a half-hour, when she felt obliged to descend again and hoped she could slip unnoticed into the drawing room. The card games were in full swing. Mrs. Granville got up as she entered. "Miss

Wren, where have you been? I have been keeping a place here for you at the whist table. I shall make my cards over to you."

"I fear she is not fond of cards," her brother came to her rescue, knowing that Kitty thought a pack of cards 'the devil's prayer book' and would suffer agonies of conscience if forced to play, especially on Christmas Night.

"Oh? Like my cousin Hewson there then, who is sitting out. He thinks us all pagans to play cards tonight."

"Kitty could entertain us at the piano," her brother added. "She is very accomplished."

Aunt Kitty noticed the Mr. Hewson referred to. He had heard the conversation.

"Capital!" he said, getting up. "To the piano then! And I shall turn the pages for you, Mrs. Wren."

They had not been properly introduced to this gentleman, and she let the mistake go.

The piano was uncovered and opened, Kitty ran her fingers over the keys and was very pleased at the mellow sound. If they could not sing carols, she could play them. She did not need music but Mr Hewson, a gentleman from Devon, stayed by her side just the same.

"I think it a bad thing to have cards on Christmas night," he whispered to her. "When my wife was alive, we used to gather around the fire, all of us including the servants, and sing carols and recite poetry. But she has gone now ten years, and my children are grown."

"A carol service is exactly what we do at home in Hetherton every Christmas night!" Kitty replied.

He continued to talk with her, and when he found out that she was the unmarried aunt, and not the mother of the children she had escorted upstairs, his manner grew warmer, and he began to talk more deeply of his faith and his heart, and it dawned upon her that she might be the object of his particular attention.

"I shall hear the children sing tomorrow before you go," he promised her when she confided the sorry tale to him, for he seemed to be a sympathetic man, a friend already.

He was as good as his word. After breakfast, he gathered a little crowd about him including their hosts and all the children and they had carol singing in the drawing room with Aunt Kitty at the piano. Mrs. Wren was very proud of her family at last, as the Granville children had not a note in their heads, though one was coaxed into reciting a poem.

AUNT KITTY FINDS LOVE

Before they left for Hetherton, Babs and Pip ran out to a frozen pond that they had spotted from their bedroom window. It had a little wilderness beside it and Babs, wandering off a little, became aware that Henry and Irene were walking there. She was so near that she overheard their conversation.

"They say that one wedding makes another," Miss Granville was saying. "I see another in the offing, do you?"

"No, I do not know what you're talking of, my dear." Henry was mystified.

"My mother's cousin Mr. Hewson, and your aunt!"

"My aunt! Aunt Kitty! Never!"

"Why, never?"

"Aunt Kitty will never marry now! She's above forty!"

"Mr. Hewson is fifty, so that will suit them well, then. And he has a grown family; it's not likely he will mind if there are no—no children."

"But how do you know this is in the offing? They only met yesterday!"

"Oh, Harry dear, nothing is known! Not yet! But the looks he gives her—tender—and her shy smile when he looks her way—it is unmistakable!"

"I have seen nothing of the kind," Henry said a little testily. "My mother needs Aunt Kitty to look after the younger ones. She can't just leave us and get married."

"Oh Harry, what a drab creature you are! Would you stand in the way of her happiness?"

"She's perfectly happy with us, Irene."

"Ah but she is not. I saw that too. Your mother orders her about."

Henry was silent. They walked on, out of hearing.

Babs was as dismayed as Henry seemed to be. She did not want Aunt Kitty to go away. She ran back to Pip, who was poking holes in the ice with a twig, and told him. But during the carriage ride home she began to change her mind. Why would Aunt Kitty not be in love and happy with her own home? By the time she had reached Hetherton, she had persuaded herself that Aunt Kitty and Mr. Hewson would be a happy couple indeed, and she might get invited to Devon to stay with them. If she was not to see Caleb and Alice anymore, that would be a holiday to look forward to.

Less than a week later the family took the road again to Whitholm, and Henry and Irene joined hands at the altar. At the reception, Mr. Hewson drew Mr. Wren aside and asked for his sister Katharine's hand in marriage, and her astonished brother gave it, if that is what Kitty wished for. And it was.

Mrs. Wren had not noticed anything at all between them and she was angry at first. But she came around.

"But Kitty, you know him so little! Have I ill-treated you, that you are desperate to get away? I was unkind to you about Babs, but I was very tense before the wedding, the worry of it, and I did not mean my words."

"That is forgotten, Gladys. But I want my own establishment. Every woman wants her own hearth."

"But do you love him?"

"I like him very much, we have the same opinions and values, which goes a long way toward love."

"But do you feel any little flutter in your breast when you think of him?"

"Well yes, as a matter of fact, I do! I cannot stop thinking of Mr. Hewson, so I must be in love!"

Babs heard these discussions and pondered them. Young as she was, the entire business of love and marriage was interesting to her. She wondered who she would marry, and whether she would love him, of course she would!

Babs helped Aunt Kitty as much as she could, for she needed new clothes and hats and she was good at sewing buttons and seams. Geoff and Pip were surprised to see their Aunt Kitty, who had always looked old and plain to them, turn into a stylish bride-to-be with a bloom to her skin and sparkling eyes.

ALICE'S PARASOL

Helping her mother and aunt took Babs's mind away from the pain of losing her friend Alice, who she had seen several times, but only in passing. Only a few short greetings had passed between them since last Christmas. She was upset, and one day she set out for the village at a time when she knew Alice went too, and caught up with her on the road. Surely a walk to the village together, when they were going the same way, was not forbidden? But something had altered between them. Alice seemed cold to her, and it hurt her, until she enquired after Caleb. Alice's face lit up.

"Our Caleb's gettin' on very well in London. Mr. Swann likes him a great deal. He delivered a long table for a Lady, a real Lady, and she was so pleased that she gave him five shillings for himself! He bought me a parasol!"

"I should love to see it!" Babs exclaimed.

"Come into the house, then, on the way home."

They did their errands together in the village and chatted happily about everything.

Thinking that Alice would be hurt if she did not go in to see her parasol, Babs entered the cottage for the first time in months. She was warmly welcomed by Mrs. Dalton, and Alice fetched the parasol from a box under her bed. It was pink in colour, and very pretty with ribbons and frills.

"When the sun comes out I'll wear it," said Alice. "But now, I don't want rain to get on it. I never 'ad anything so pretty in all my life!"

All chill between them had melted away. She told them all about Aunt Kitty's preparations for the wedding and they promised that they would be in the church to see her on the day itself.

When she reached home, her mother was too distracted to question her about where she had been, because her mind was occupied elsewhere. They were to provide the hospitality for Aunt Kitty's wedding. Even her father was tetchy and ordered the house to be painted and several repairs to be done.

"I am heartily sick of this Granville connection." Fourteen-year-old Geoff complained to Babs and Pip after his father told him he could not buy him a cricket bat. "Nothing good is coming of it. Now we have to spend more than we have to spend, in order to keep up the appearance of being wealthy, and we're not wealthy. Father is as bad as Mother."

LAVISH—AND FOOLISH

Every penny was going into smartening up the house to make the family look wealthier than they were. New furnishings, new carpet for the guest apartments, hangings for the dining room, and silver enough to serve thirty people at table. Babs noticed that Aunt Kitty, the bride-to-be, was not the centre of attention anymore—her mother was obsessed with how the house was looking and how good the fare would be that they would be expected to provide. She put the tradesmen in an uproar. The butcher came in for her sharp tongue; the baker told her to go to Paris for the cake. Candles and lamps were rejected at the chandlers, deemed to be plain and provincial. The guest soaps had to be ordered by post, and she would have to go to London to be sure of getting anything nice at all. They went deeply into debt, and Aunt Kitty was humiliated that it was upon her account that this show was taking place. She pleaded for a small, quiet wedding—but no, the Wrens had to provide as good or better than they had received at Whitholm, especially since she was marrying one of the family.

Mr. Hewson returned to Essex for the wedding. It took place on a sunny day and Mrs. Dalton and Alice were in the church with many other villagers who wanted to wish the couple well. Alice twirled her parasol outside the church. But Babs, under the eye of her mother, could not run up to her and tell her how lovely it looked in the sunshine, especially with the Granvilles present. The invited guests proceeded to the Wren house to partake of a lavish wedding breakfast. Henry and Irene, married three months now, looked very happy, though Henry bewailed to Mr. Burlington, his father's partner in business, about all the work he had to do administering the Granville Estate.

The newlyweds took off for Devon that same afternoon.

Babs was very lonely for Aunt Kitty. Her lessons ceased. She played the piano, practicing as if Aunt Kitty would come in any moment and ask to hear her. There was talk of sending her to school, but nothing came of it. The bills began to pour in.

"Henry marrying Miss Granville was supposed to be a wonderful thing," Geoff grumbled again. "But it's only caused us to become strapped for cash! What is the advantage of marrying into a rich family if you end up not being able to afford anything?"

CHRISTMAS POVERTY

Mr. Wren's financial troubles were not easily resolved but he thought that with careful economy he might recoup what he lost in time. But his business partner Mr. Burlington was growing anxious about Wren's financial situation. There were men from the City's financial district waiting for Wren when he came back from lunch, and he could hear arguments behind his office doors. Mr. Burlington thought he had better leave while the business was still solvent and begin again elsewhere. When he went to the bank, he found that Mr. Wren had taken loans from the business without consulting him. Great loans in the hundreds of pounds. He went home and considered his situation. He then forged his partner's signature on documents dissolving the company and having repaid the loans took all the remaining funds out of the bank, packed his suitcases and left London for good.

Mr. Wren arrived at the office one Monday morning in May to find a crew of workmen removing the furniture, his sign being painted over and no trace of his partner. The landlord told him that the company was dissolved—Mr. Burlington had told him so. A hurried trip to the Bank made all clear—everything was gone. The company was no more—he had nothing except his many debts. Debts to the same bank due on his personal account.

He returned home and taking Mrs. Wren to his library where he kept all his business documents, explained the situation to her. She did not understand.

"All? You mean, all the money is gone? That is ridiculous, Stephen."

"We have no money left, Gladys."

"There surely is enough for our necessities! What about the lamp for the dining room, the one we have is very old-fashioned, I was ashamed of it opposite the Granvilles."

"With what will you buy it, Gladys? There is *no money*. We cannot even pay the servants. Turn them off straightaway." He was shouting, and finally the penny dropped. Mrs. Wren looked at him, horror-stricken. Her husband sat at the desk and groaned, a great, deep suffering groan.

"We should not have spent so much," he lamented. "Oh Gladys, we have been very, very foolish!"

"There must be some redress!" Mrs Wren sat by him, her face ashen.

"None at all. We cannot stay here."

"Leave our house? No, dear."

"We must sell. Turn off the carriage, sell the horses, the linens and the silver. We will have no use for them in the future, in any case. The proceeds from the sale will have to pay our debts so that I am in good standing to get capital for another business. We will live frugally until we get on our feet again."

"But the Granvilles... where shall we entertain our relatives..." her voice trailed away. Her husband's silence was her answer.

Babs had drawn close to hear the conversation, and since neither parent had sent her away, she listened intently. They were going to be poor.

"Papa, will we be as poor as the Daltons?" she asked.

"Perhaps for a few years," he said. Mrs. Wren shook her head vehemently.

"Never!" cried her mother.

But she had to face the reality of what they were now. Penniless.

Babs was too young to understand what this change meant, but her thought was that she could be friends with the Daltons again. Now they could all go about together again like they used to before. The boys would not return to school in the autumn and they would have to work.

The house went up for sale. But there were few interested, and as winter approached the family found themselves living in its cold shell. The servants were gone, as was most of the furniture. They could only afford fuel enough to heat one room, so they ate in the warm kitchen and sat there for the evenings before retiring to their cold bedrooms.

People react to disaster in unexpected ways. It was Mrs. Wren who, after a week of anger and then of a deep meditative silence which alarmed everybody, accepted the situation. She told Babs later that when she was a child, she had read The Book of Job, and during her week of silence it had come back to her, impressing itself upon her in a deep way. Her snobbishness and extravagance and paranoia about what people thought of her had played a large part in this disaster. Job had been innocent—he had been tried anyway. She had not been innocent and now had to reform herself and try to patch it all up again. And poor Papa, he had been guilty as well! Now he was paralysed with a melancholy that deepened every week that the house was not sold. The railways now reached beyond the City in every direction, and men of business could live wherever they wished. Hetherton lost popularity. The only offers came from a Mr. Pratt, an unscrupulous opportunist who Mr. Wren detested, as he was offering a ridiculously low price for the house.

CHRISTMAS CONSOLATIONS

Babs mastered the range and cooked and baked with her mother. They became closer than they had ever been as they worked together running the house—their little part of it—and Babs felt she was important to her now, whereas she had never felt that before. They talked of many things. She learned for the first time that her mother had had a very lonely childhood, raised by her strict grandmother after her parents died. Great-grandmamma had instilled into Gladys the importance of having an elevated place in society and nothing else really mattered to her. She had been very cross when Gladys had refused to marry a titled gentleman because she had fallen in love with Mr. Wren.

"Now I see how wrong she was, Babs. My dear, during this time we've talked about many things, haven't we? It hasn't been all bad, has it? This dreadful thing that happened to us? We're alive. And I never noticed that Alice has a lovely smile, her eyes sparkle, don't they?" For Alice came and went from the house as she pleased now. The two girls were the best of friends again and Mrs. Wren was always warm and friendly to the girl she had thought not good enough to be friends with her daughter. Alice forgave her quickly. But Alice was leaving soon to go into service as a kitchen maid far away in Colchester.

Christmas came, and there was still no sale. It was a meagre time. The Granvilles sent a goose and a hamper. Their fall was well known to them now. But none visited; not even Henry rode over from Whitholm to see his family and to express sorrow at their situation. He could have done so much, but he seemed to have washed his hands of them.

But Caleb Dalton called upon them on Christmas Eve. He was the same old Chippy Dalton, natural and kind. He joked with them as if he had never left for the City, though he entertained them with plenty of strange tales from there.

After the Christmas service at church, Mrs. Wren sat her children down in the kitchen and spoke with them. Their father had gone for a walk. He went for long walks and never wanted anybody's company.

"Nobody would want our trouble, children. We have no gifts for you this Christmas. We know you understand.

But I wish to tell you something. This has been a hard year for us, but it has been astounding for your father and myself to see how resilient, how generous, how understanding our children have been about this dreadful fall into what we hope is temporary poverty. Not one of you has asked for anything beyond food, and I hope we have enough of that. Pip, you are always first down in the morning and have the fire lighting."

"I can't sleep in the cold," grinned Pip, embarrassed.

"Geoff, you're not too proud to herd Farmer Dickson's cattle, or to clean the stables for Reverend James."

"I like to be busy, Mother," Geoff said, smiling, though his face was red also.

"And Babs—it is a gift to me to be with you as we are now, my best daughter."

"You don't have another to compare me with, Mama!" Babs was embarrassed also, but very pleased.

"So, I have the best children in the world. If only—but Henry has his own problems perhaps, and we will not judge Henry."

"Mama, is Father going to be all right?" Geoff asked her.

"Yes, he will be all right, if we can sell the house."

"Perhaps he will sell to Mr. Pratt after all."

"I hope not, for Mr. Pratt belongs to a class of entrepreneurs who buy cheap and then sell for twice that much when the market changes."

"I hope he returns before the goose is roasted; because I don't want to have to wait!" Pip said, because the range was beginning to give off delicious aromas.

"Is that me you are talking of?" their father came in. He had a smile upon his face. His face was purple from the cold. His hands were blue. "Look, I have something for you all." He held up a tin of cocoa.

They had a welcome hot drink to cheer them, and Babs noticed that he was without his gloves. Had he sold them, to buy the cocoa?

They had a good dinner, and at dusk they sang carols in the warm kitchen. They were not hungry—it was something to thank God for. They had fuel—another blessing. They had each other, and all had grown in affection for each other in the last hard months. That was the best of all. Another round of hot cocoa followed, after which they said goodnight to each other and climbed the freezing stairs to their equally freezing bedchambers. Babs fell asleep immediately, the carols still echoing in her head as she burrowed into bed, drawing the covers around about her until she was in a warm cocoon of her own making. On Boxing Day, they again had good food, and visited the Daltons. The young people went for a long tramp in the frosty lanes and fields and afterwards drank cocoa in the Wren kitchen. Geoff and Pip went to look for work on the farms the following day; for the winter was a lean time and the farms had their own dairy hands to milk cows and tend the animals.

Babs went about with her friends Alice and Caleb Dalton and the Bates and Tarrant children. She looked up to Caleb Dalton. Handsome, confident, kind Caleb. He went back to London on New Year's Day.

FROM BAD TO WORSE

Spring came in slowly, and the house began to lose its chill. Babs was very anxious about her father—he seemed to live in another world far away from them. But in February, the house was sold at last, but it was to the persistent Mr. Pratt who purchased it for half its worth. The family moved into a small cottage outside the village for a low rent. It was drab and dusty. Babs and her mother set to work to put it to rights, and with hard work it began to look like home. Her mother now had to draw water from a well and cook over an open fire like the other cottagers.

"That's who we are now," Mrs Wren said. "Cottagers. If my grandmother only knew! She would think we were better off dead, but I know we're not."

There was now no contact with Whitholm. Henry might as well be in another country.

Mr. Wren used the money from the sale to provide capital to set up a new business. A premises was rented, office furniture bought, merchandise imported, and the boys began to assist in the business. They set off for London every day for six months. At the end of that time Mr. Wren had to admit that it was a failure. He closed. He was now a desperate, bitter man and difficult to live with. Babs saw that the Papa of her earlier years had been replaced by a very sad and angry man.

Geoff and Pip went back to their labouring jobs in the farms around the district.

"What shall we do with you, Babs?" her mother said to her one day.

"Do with me? What do you mean, Mama?"

"I think we will send you off to your Aunt Kitty, in Devon. She needs help with the baby."

To everybody's astonishment, Aunt Kitty had borne a child. But her advanced age at her first delivery had made the birth very difficult and had left her in poor health. The girl-child was healthy, however, and her pride and joy.

Whereas two years before Babs would have leaped at the chance to spend her life with Aunt Kitty, it was very different now. She and her mother had become much closer, and her heart was with her, her father and her brothers. She had often thanked God that she had not been sent away to school but had been able to be at home working with her mother. She felt needed by her and by her father.

She was growing up and wondering if she was pretty. Especially at Christmas and for two weeks in August when Caleb was at home. She had pimples that spoiled her complexion. Her mother told her to be patient and she would grow out of them.

"I don't wish to go to Devon," Babs declared. "But Mama, I know I have to do something; I have to earn money, like the boys, and like Alice. I will go to Colchester too, into domestic service."

But she was unprepared for her father's strong objection.

"No!" he cried out. "Babs, you will not go into service; I forbid it. I can keep my wife and daughter. What kind of man am I, if I can't keep my wife and my only daughter?"

He was trembling with emotion, and her mother signalled to her not to pursue the matter. She ladled some thin stew onto her plate. Their fare now was barely adequate. Mr. Wren did not seem to understand that they had hardly enough for the necessities of life. He himself ate very little, wandered off on his walks without mufflers or gloves, and slept fitfully. He had a gaunt figure, and his face was deeply lined. He spent his days planning new schemes, hopeless dreams of making money and getting back on his feet. Babs knew that her mother had a difficult time listening to these unrealistic plans and that her father had become a dependent on her mother. Mrs. Wren took in washing and pretended that they were doing charity work for some of the older neighbours and their father either did not see the deception or preferred not to see it.

VANISHED

November was very wet and windy. There was a storm one night, and Babs woke up suddenly. She was sure she had heard the front door bang. She went out—it had indeed blown open and a gale was blowing through the cottage. She shut it, but not without becoming drenched. She went back to bed after drying herself off, and the storm abated.

The following morning, she was awakened early by Geoff and Pip before they went out to the farms.

"Where are Mama and Papa?" they asked.

She sat up suddenly in bed.

"Why? What's the matter?"

"They're not here—did you hear them go out?"

She sprang from her bed and pulled a shawl about her.

"The door swung open some hours ago, I went out and shut it."

"Were they here then?"

"I don't know!"

"Was their door opened or closed?"

"I didn't see! I didn't think of looking!"

She sped into her parents' small bedroom. The covers were thrown back exposing the sheet. The sheet was cold to touch.

"They haven't been in it for some time," she said. "Oh, where can they have got to?"

"We have to look for them," Geoff said. He was already dressed and went out onto the road, followed by Pip, who went in the opposite direction. Babs got dressed hurriedly and went to their nearest neighbours to find out if they had been seen.

But nobody had seen them. Geoff, Pip and Babs searched and enquired all day long. Before long the villagers were out too, searching sheds, old barns and even looking about the banks of the stream to see if there was any sign of Mr and Mrs. Wren. The constable was informed; he notified nearby villages, and the constables there kept a lookout. On the third day the vicar held a prayer service for their safe return. Bets was distraught. The consensus among the villagers was that they had met with some great misadventure—perhaps slipped into the river at the point where it was deep and ran rapidly over hidden rocks. Ma Haydock, Hetherton's oldest resident who was reckoned to be past ninety, said she had seen a flock of ravens, a very unlucky sign, circle over that place only a short time before.

"In a week or two, their bodies will wash up along the bank," whispered the villagers to each other.

"Poor Mr. Wren—he couldn't take poverty. He went into the river and Mrs. Wren followed to save him—and was lost. Both are lost."

Others said that they had run away, leaving their children to fend for themselves. After all, the boys were grown and Babs well of an age to go to work. The couple went to build themselves a new life somewhere.

The rumours reached the children.

"They didn't run off," Babs said firmly. "But that leaves the other thing they're saying—I don't want to believe that either! No! Mama and Papa are not dead!"

"We should inform Henry," Geoff said. "I'm the eldest, I'll do it."

HENRY'S PLAN

The boys had been paying the rent for some time now, and there was no threat of eviction. Babs kept house and did the cooking and took in more washing.

One Sunday afternoon a fashionable carriage clattered up the village street and halted at their ramshackle gate. It was after dinner and Babs was pouring the dirty dishwater out into the grassy patch beside the door. The door was therefore open, and the occupant was immediately seen by her brothers.

"It's Henry!" Geoff and Pip chorused together.

"He must have news!" Babs exclaimed. "Oh, that they are alive, and he is looking after them! That must be it!" She threw the basin to one side with a clatter and ran to him as her brothers dashed out of the house.

He did not seem pleased to see them, and fear struck them. Whatever the news was, it was not going to be to their liking. He dismounted, and before saying anything, he looked up and down at the humble abode of his brothers and sister and shook his head.

"To have come down to this," he said.

"Henry! What news have you? Did you get our letter?"

"Oh, please Henry, tell us—what is it? Are they alive? Are they found?"

"I can tell you nothing of our parents," he said testily. "Except that they are *not* dead. They are safe. I have come to tell you what to do now. As the eldest of the family, I have made some decisions which I will now tell you about."

It was a relief to hear that their parents were alive, but very frustrating that Henry was mute on every other point concerning them.

"Well come in then," Geoff said crossly, for he did not like Henry's manner and tone.

When Henry entered the cottage, it seemed to become twice as poor as it was beforehand. He looked about, frowned, squinted in the semi-darkness, and sat reluctantly in the best chair.

"Tea! We were just about to have tea," Babs said.

"No, thank you," he said.

"Where are Mama and Papa, Henry? Where could they be? What do you think happened to them?"

"Do not ask me," he said. "But this is what you have to do. I have money for you, Geoff, to go to America." He put his hand into his inside pocket and pulled out a long white envelope.

"America!" chorused all the younger members of the family.

"It is the best thing, and as the eldest member of the family, I am not suggesting it, I am ordering it." Henry said. "That is your fare and money to live on until you begin to earn. There are ample opportunities for you to work there. You should get a job as soon as your feet hit the ground. When you have enough money saved, you can send for Philip and Barbara. Until then, Philip and Barbara will live at Whitholm."

There was quiet in the cottage. Geoffry did not move.

"Well, take it!" Henry said impatiently. Geoff held out his hand and took the envelope.

"Now you younger two—get your things," Henry said a little impatiently. "I haven't all day, have I?"

"Now?" Babs said. Everything was happening too fast. She did not want to leave here in case her mother and father should return. She felt suddenly alone and afraid to leave this cottage and Hetherton.

"Now!" Henry said crossly.

"Why can't Pip come to America with me?" Geoff asked. "Take Babs with you to Whitholm, she will be safer there. But let Pip come with me."

"No, that's not possible," Henry said. "Philip is to stay."

Tears began to gather in Babs's eyes as reality dawned. Her parents were missing, and she had no idea when they would return. All was changed. She laid her head on her arms on the table and cried great sobs.

"Don't take on, sister," Pip said tenderly patting her shoulder. "We mustn't lose hope about anything."

Henry gave an exasperated sigh.

"Come on, Babs. Get your things. Put on your best gown to meet the Granvilles."

"This is my best gown," Babs snivelled.

Henry sighed.

"And you, Philip? Is—is that your Sunday best also?" Henry looked him up and down with dread.

"Yes, it is."

Henry sighed again. "This is a great deal worse than I thought," he said gloomily.

"Am I to go to Whitholm first?" Geoff said, holding the envelope in his hand and turning it over.

"There's no necessity for that. You're closer to London here than at Whitholm. Say your goodbyes, get on the next train, ask directions to the White Star shipping office, book your ticket to New York, and you'll be working and earning and making scads of money in a matter of days. I wish I was you. I wish I was going. The ships are steam now, and it's said to be a ripping voyage, lucky you, with the best of food and drink. That said, that's a steerage fare you have in the envelope. Work hard and you'll soon be a wealthy man."

Geoff seemed to be coming around to this idea. Getting an envelope full of money was presenting all kinds of opportunities to his mind and his eyes were growing bigger and rounder as Henry gave his little speech. America! Money! Wealth? He held up the envelope.

"Is there enough in here to pay for food on the ship?" he asked.

"Food is included, as is a bed," Henry said in an exasperated tone. "A bed to yourself, what's more. Luxury."

Pip helped Babs up and encouraged her to pack her clothes. They were pitifully few and very shabby. His were those of a farm labourer—two smock-frocks and leggings. He had one pair of boots and a 'good' suit for Sundays, which he was wearing. The sleeves and trouser legs were too short. He crammed his cap upon his head, and Babs tied her bonnet under her chin and put on her shawl.

"Well goodbye, Geoff," Pip said, sticking out his hand, his heart full of emotion at this sudden parting.

Geoff shook his hand as if in a dream.

"Oh Geoff, do look after yourself, and write as soon as you land in New York!" Babs was not restrained in her farewell. She threw her arms about her brother and burst into fresh tears as he hugged her tight.

"Look after yourself, little sister. Pip, look after her." His face was flushed and full of emotion.

So that's why Pip isn't going, Babs thought suddenly. *Henry is not going to be responsible for me—he wants Pip to do that.*

Babs was right, but it had not been Henry who had made the decision.

Henry had wanted to send both brothers to America but Mr and Mrs. Granville had disagreed. Afraid of a future when they would be expected to absorb Barbara into the home and provide for her indefinitely (and who would marry her without a fortune?) they knew that Philip would in time fulfil the role of protector.

The goodbyes complete, the carriage took the three off to Whitholm as Geoff stood out on the road and looked after it, clutching the precious envelope and still amazed at the alteration that one short hour could bring to one's life. The villagers came to him. They had been afraid to come while Henry was present.

"I'm going to America," Geoff said, still bewildered.

LIVING AT WHITHOLM

They reached Whitholm after dark. The butler was disdainful of this pathetic pair who entered the front door and were shown into the drawing room.

"Well, children, though you are children no longer," Mrs. Granville said without getting up. "You are welcome. We are so very sorry to hear of the loss of your parents. We hope you will be happy here with us. Nell will show you to your quarters and you will settle in—and dinner is served at eight."

She pulled the bell and a maid appeared a few moments later.

"Nell, show the young people to the attic rooms."

"Attic rooms, Madam?"

"Yes, the two empty attic rooms."

Henry looked down, ashamed.

At first, two guest rooms had been assigned, but when Mrs. Granville saw the pair, she changed her mind. The youth looked like a street urchin, and the girl was dressed no better than a servant in a very low establishment. Having seen them before dressed as befitting their rank then, it was a shock to realise just how far the family had fallen into ruin. Henry should have been more honest! It would not do for them to live with the family. She was sure that they were dirty and full of fleas. She would have to speak to the housekeeper and arrange baths and delousings, and their clothes would have to burnt. They could not sit with them at table.

The housekeeper, cross and flustered, came to them and told them they were to bathe. The disgruntled maids hauled buckets of hot water to the tin bath in the servants' quarters and Babs had hers first, followed by Pip. He was angry and offended. Babs then had her hair examined.

"Why it's clean," said the housemaid, having examined it at arm's length with a snooty expression on her face.

"Of course, it's clean!" Babs said crossly, tears standing in her eyes.

In his little room the footman was examining Pip's head and came to the same conclusion. Pip ordered him out.

"I don't need a nurse," he snapped. "Go away." The footman departed and told his story to the butler, who decided that the boy he had been told to call 'Master Philip' was not deserving of that title. It was time for dinner; he struck the gong, and the family gathered in the drawing room.

Henry was upset that Philip and Barbara were not there. It reflected badly upon him. He asked Mrs. Granville what arrangements had been made for their evening repast.

"I think that for the moment they would feel very uncomfortable with us," she answered smoothly. "When they have settled in, they will join us, but for now, I think it's best they eat with the servants."

"I agree," said Mr. Granville.

Henry was mortified. His wife Irene looked at him with concern. She loved him perhaps more than he had loved her at first, but she was confident that now she had his heart. He enjoyed the cosiness of marriage, and they were expecting a baby. She made sure that her parents treated him with respect and that he was never taunted about his poverty, for having lost his birthright, the Hetherton house and the land with it. He had nothing of his own.

In her attic room Babs was trying to sleep. But so many thoughts and feelings ran about in her head that it was next to impossible. She had not liked this house when she had come here for Christmas before; she liked it even less now.

"Surely we can't stay here," she whispered to Pip as they ate their breakfast the following morning in the servant's hall.

"We must stay for a time at least, for if we leave, where shall we go? If Mama and Papa are found, how would we ever know about it?" Pip answered. "If there is any news of them, the news will reach here. We must bide here for a while, Babs."

UNHAPPINESS

After three days they were allowed to join the family for meals, at Irene's insistence. She loved their brother, and her love extended to his family. They had been outfitted with hand-me-downs from the Granville children. Irene was larger than Babs, so her gowns were ill-fitting. She would have to take them in. Pip fared better; he had Henry's castoffs and they were much the same size. They had to be found occupations; Pip was to accompany Henry on his daily tour of farm and cottages; Babs was to sew with the women if they were not going out to pay calls. She heartily wished they would be out every morning so that she did not have to endure Mrs. Granville's company. She missed her mother greatly and was silent in her grief.

"You should abandon that sullen countenance of yours," Mrs. Granville said. "It makes me feel ill. Irene's child will be born melancholy and upset with the world."

Christmas approached. But the festive season was not to be found in their young hearts. They were unhappy. Pip thought that he would go to London and seek his fortune there. Surely it would be better than here?

"Why do we not go back to Hetherton?" Babs asked. Caleb would be there at Christmastime. She thought about him and wondered if he ever thought of her. Why would he? She was a girlish fifteen with a pimply face, and he was tall and twenty with a head of thick, wavy fair hair. She imagined London to be filled with beautiful girls who would capture his heart. She still had his mouth organ, she treasured it.

"Where would we stay at Hetherton?" Pip asked. "We can't ask anybody to put us up—they're as poor as us, and we have no money to pay lodgings. Nobody goes to the country to find work, they go to the City. I'll go to London. We're an embarrassment to our brother here."

"Don't go without me," Babs implored him.

"I'm not even sure I'll go yet. What if news comes of Mama and Papa? How will we know? You're better off here, Babs. But I'm sixteen and I can find my own way."

"Don't leave me here," Babs implored. "The family have no regard for me, only Irene has any consideration for me. The servants sneer. If you leave on your own, I will run away."

"We'll go together, then, if you're so unhappy."

BABS TAKES CHARGE

In December the house was decorated with trees and sparkling lights and expensive decorations, for the Granvilles had invited several friends from London to the country for Christmas. The Barrett family were the first to arrive on Christmas Eve in two handsome carriages. The men were smartly dressed, and the women swathed in furs.

Babs was in the hall when they arrived. It was an accidental meeting—she had occasion to find Henry to ask him if he had any news of their parents. She sought him out and asked him every day. The answer was always an impatient 'no' followed by an irritated remark to the effect that if he had any news for her, he would have told her.

Occupied with her own thoughts, she encountered the Barretts in the hall, but as she did not wear a servant's uniform or curtsy, but simply stared at them in surprise, they did not know what to make of her. Mrs. Granville appeared in a hurry and introduced her as 'Miss Barbara' who was a distant relative, an orphan who they had taken in. "She is simple-minded, you must excuse her," Babs heard Mrs. Granville explain as she hurried her guests to the drawing room. Babs slipped away, disgusted. Soon after, she heard the other guests arrive—a collection of noisy young men, friends of Frederick, who arrived with them, and more couples, young and middle-aged.

As darkness fell, the company was complete, and they gathered for dinner. Babs and Pip took their places. She had told Pip what Mrs Granville had said, and they were determined to look as well as they could and to make superior conversation. Babs's manners were impeccable, and Mrs. Barrett, sitting opposite her, thought her very well-trained for a simpleton. Pips engaged his neighbour with a discussion about the lost Franklin Expedition, a subject that had interested his father for years.

When the ladies withdrew to the drawing room, Babs went straight to the grand piano. She had noticed before dinner that it was open. Taking a deep breath to give herself courage, she sat down and began to softly play an old French carol Aunt Kitty had taught her. She was a little out of practice but soon her fingers flew about the keys in a familiar way, and she began to sing the carol, in perfect French, softly as if to herself. The room fell silent; her voice became stronger; someone hushed a chattering duo. When she had finished Irene exclaimed, "That is exquisite, dear sister! Do play something else!"

"It is very pretty indeed, but hardly an Oratorio," smirked a good friend of Mrs. Granville's.

In response, Babs took another deep breath. She knew a little classical Christmas work and while she did not execute Handel's 'For unto us a Child is Born' perfectly, it was very good and everybody listened. She had no music in front of her—she had memorised this! Mrs. Barrett raised an eyebrow and looked quizzically at Mrs. Granville, who looked down at the rug at her feet. Irene beamed.

The gentlemen came in during this, and were equally amazed, for they had been informed that she was of very low intelligence. The host family looked foolish indeed, and Pip was laughing silently to himself. Good old Babs! Nothing could keep her down!

"Well done!" Irene said, and Henry, whose first feeling was embarrassment at his sister making an exhibition of herself, then looked happy and proud of her.

That did away with any impression that she was as Mrs. Granville had described her. A simpleton could not play as she could.

The tone had been set for the evening. A woman asked for the carol from Austria—*Stille Nacht*. Did anybody know it? One of the young gentlemen nodded—he was a good tenor and sang it feelingly in German. One carol followed another until the tea-things were brought in.

The only unhappy people present were the host couple.

"You may not wish to take part in the Christmas festivities as you are in mourning," Mrs. Granville addressed her the following morning.

"My parents are not dead, Ma'am," she said quietly. "Wherever they may be, I know they wish us to celebrate the Holy Season."

AN UNHOLY CHRISTMAS

But Christmas in Whitholm was not a holy occasion. Though everybody went to Church the following day, they returned to a breakfast where the wine began to flow and people became tipsy even before dinner. Expensive gifts were exchanged, and the women showed off the jewellery that their husbands had bought them. There were no gifts for Pip or Babs, nor did they give any—they had nothing of their own. Only Irene had thought of them. She had given Babs a ballgown of deep blue, apologising all the while that it was not new, and seeing that Henry had nothing for his brother Pip, had found a watch-chain that had belonged to her grandfather and gave it to him.

Dinner was lavish and a dance followed in the ballroom. Babs knew there would not be any carols sung. She put on her ballgown; like everything of Irene's, it did not fit her properly, but there was no time to alter it. At least the colour suited her. She and Pip went downstairs to join the party.

What she witnessed in the course of the evening appalled her. A married woman slunk upstairs with one of Frederick's bachelor friends, and a couple not married to each other whispered and held hands in a corner. Their spouses were similiarly engaged with others. Wine and spirits continued to flow, glasses were everywhere, full, half-full, empty, knocked over on tables, staining the white cloths. Most of the people were drunk. Pip was persuaded to drink more than he should by Mr. Granville and he fell asleep on a sofa. When he awoke he went upstairs to bed.

One of Frederick's friends pursued her all night. He tried to kiss her on the dance floor, and her brother Henry looked on and did nothing. This man, Claude, followed her upstairs later, and came into her attic room without knocking. She had just loosened her hair and looked at him in no little alarm.

"I say is this where you sleep? It's awful. They treat you badly, don't they? Come to my room instead. There's a fire there."

"You are drunk!"

"I won't ruin you," he said. "Do let us lie together—we can talk, and no harm done, you know, and you can slip back here later on. All the married women are at it with other men, if they get with child, it will be all right for them, but I promise you I will do nothing like that."

"You tell a lie, they are not all 'at it' as you put it, there are some morally upright women who are in love with their husbands."

He laughed. "All right, I exaggerated. But I have nobody tonight. Do come to me. I am in the second room on the right after the bust of Apollo, I will leave the door a little ajar."

Thankfully he took 'no' for an answer and he left her alone.

This was Christmas Night among the richest and most respected people in the district. Babs sank to her knees in her ballgown and tried to put it out of her head. She thought of her warm and cosy childhood Christmasses at Hetherton, but the family was now broken and lost. She thought of the Dalton cottage and its inhabitants and their neighbours popping in to wish them a Merry Christmas and to ask Caleb how he was getting on in London. She thought of the village church and Vespers by candlelight where people worshipped the Newborn King. And where was Geoff? He was alone too, in a strange land, was he alone at Christmas? If so, he was even worse off than she and Pip.

She worshipped and adored Jesus for a time in her cold attic room. How abandoned He was in this house! As she prayed, the thought came to her that they must be empty, sad people and that God wanted her to pray for them instead of concentrating upon how bad they were behaving.

The following morning only a few guests appeared for breakfast. Pip was there and she could not be cross with him; he had a severe headache and acknowledged that perhaps Mr. Granville had tried to make a fool of him.

"Did you have a good time last night, Miss Wren?" asked Mrs. Barrett. "You were in demand."

Babs looked around for Claude. He was not there. She avoided him all day. Thankfully he left the day after Boxing Day.

After New Year's all the guests departed. In this time some of the ladies had taken the time to get to know Miss Wren better. As she said goodbye, one of them, a bright young thing who appeared to be a great flirt, said to her:

"Miss Wren, the best part—the most enjoyable part—of this entire visit was Christmas Eve in the drawing room. I wish there had been more attention paid to—to that side of things. You know what I mean."

Babs smiled. There was a hunger in this woman's heart. No amount of flirting or champagne could satisfy that longing.

"I hope you find your mother and father," this woman said then, pressing her hands.

"Pray that I will," asked Babs impulsively. The woman laughed at first, before saying: "I haven't prayed for years; but I will now."

TO LONDON

Mr. Granville called his son-in-law to his office to see him. Henry wondered what he had done now—made an error in accounting?

"Your relatives cannot stay," he said abruptly. "My wife is not happy with your sister. She is impertinent and has no function here."

"She is a friend of my wife's," Harry spoke up for both women, for he was pleased to see Irene attach herself to his sister.

"It does not signify. They must leave soon."

"They have nothing, sir."

"Then give them something!"

Henry left the room, unhappy. He hated being caught between relatives like this—it was the worst situation in the world. He had a little money, it was true, but that was not for his brother and sister—it was to enable him to keep up with his in-laws. Once more he bitterly regretted the loss of the Hetherton House—the one that was to have been his. He and Irene could have moved there and been happy. He was not happy, in spite of having a loving wife. Having his brother and sister around as dependents made his position difficult.

He was therefore distant with them. They could not fail to notice. A letter arrived from New York—they were seized with excitement, but it was some hours before Henry told them that Geoff had found work and was saving for their tickets to join him.

"I hope it will not be long," he said, "for my in-laws' sake."

"He wants us gone," Pip said later. "We're a burden and an embarrassment."

"Then we shall go," Bets declared. "To London, then. Isn't that what we agreed? We will make our own way there, Pip. I will go into service or something and you, being a man, will have your pick of occupations."

They left the following week when the weather became a little better. They had no money and left everything behind them except the clothes they wore and one change. It was a long walk to London; they suffered cold and hunger, and slept outside a couple of nights when there was no shed or barn to shelter in. They reached the outskirts of the city one cold evening and begged at a farmhouse for food. They were given a little hot broth and stale bread and slept in the barn, then the following day—London, which had become the Promised Land in their eyes, surely a land of plenty, of milk and honey, was gained. They did not know how deep into London they were, for the farther they walked, the more populous the roads and streets, and then suddenly they seemed to be in the country again and were puzzled, but gradually the green spaces gave way to continuous streets, carriages, carts, walkers, and industry. They were there, in the great metropolis of the British Empire, where wealth was made. They walked on, and Babs's eyes kept darting about.

"What are you looking about so much for?" Pip asked.

"Swanns Furniture," was the reply.

"Oh, Caleb Dalton! But we're not likely to stumble on it, Babs. London's very big."

"I know."

"We have to look for work without delay," Pip said then. "Because nobody is going to come up to us and offer it."

"I'm going to ask at this house," Babs said, and knocked on the front door. But she was turned away at house after house and, after an hour, thought that they would have to find another way. So, they turned to the merchants—but had no success there either.

THE QUARREL

"From the country, I suppose," one greengrocer said to them after they had begged him, their pride firmly put away as they outlined their desperation. "Why you country folks think London is going to give you a livin' the hour you get 'ere, I don't know. That's 'ow the workhouses are full. And you don't 'ave a trade—" this was to Pip, "—and you don't 'ave characters, Miss, you 'ave no 'ope of getting anything. 'Ere, take an apple each and off with you. I'm busy."

"The workhouse, Babs." Pip said firmly as they walked on.

"The workhouse, Pip! Are we really going to a workhouse?"

"Not me, Babs. You."

"Me! Why? Why me?"

"I'm responsible for you and I'd get work faster if I was alone. When I'm up and running, I'll come and fetch you from there. Come on, you have to agree, Babs. It's the only way."

"I didn't come to London to go to the workhouse," Babs argued. The very idea of having to join the poorest, lowest people in society was horrific to her. How would she ever recover from such a place? How would she ever explain it to anybody?

They had a quarrel, voices raised in between bites of their apples.

"See it my way, Babs. I can't leave you here on the streets while I go down to the factories and docklands to get work. That's where the work is, I bet."

"I will be fine here," Babs retorted. "Maybe I'll find it easier to get work without you tagging along."

"What if you don't? You'll be alone on the streets. No girl should be alone on the streets, I won't have my sister exposed like that, in a strange city in the dark, with all kinds of ruffians and drunks pouring out of the public houses, and not a friend to call on in all of London, and no money for a cab even if you knew somebody. I won't be responsible for it, I won't. You at least have to be looked after and in a safe place."

Pip, not a tall lad, seemed to have grown two inches as he made that speech. Babs was silent. She saw his concern, his care, and her anger melted. He ate his apple, core and all and spat out the pips.

Finally, she saw a way.

"Very well then, Pip. I will do as you say. I will go to the workhouse but only for a time. A short time."

"I will take you there, then."

"How do we find one?"

"I have no idea."

"We have to ask somebody."

So, they did. The answer was supplied readily—Brownton workhouse was not far away. They turned their steps toward it and Pip took his sister by the elbow and steered her toward the porter's gate.

"My sister is indigent," he said. "She needs admission."

"Indigent, is she? Why can't you keep 'er? A big strong bloke loike you?"

"I 'aven't a job, have I?" Pip, no doubt fearing that Babs would be turned away, took a step backward.

"I'll come back for you when I have somewhere for us to live," he said, anxious to beat a hasty retreat. "Goodbye, little sister."

"Don't leave me!" Babs was seized with terror. She had

lost her entire family except for Pip and now he was going away also. She burst into tears.

"I have to, little sister." He never called her 'little sister,' but she understood it was to make clear to her that he was in charge of her. He had the responsibility. He gave her a quick hug.

"This way, girl." The porter steered her inside. Pip strode quickly away in case the porter changed his mind.

BROWNTON WORKHOUSE

The workhouse was the very last place Babs expected to be on her first full night in London. An inmate in that dreaded place, where only the destitute went and as a last resort.

Brownton was a dull and towering building with thick walls and airless rooms. The deeper she went into its hidden parts, the more anxious she felt. It was almost as if she had gone underground into a series of tunnels. It was dusk and the attendants carried flickering candles as they flitted about their business. The windows were high up in the walls, the corridors long and suffocating, the smells were overwhelming—ere of disinfectant, there of bodily odours, another of dampness, and nothing pleasant to see, to hear or to please any of the senses. As she was led along, doors clanking behind her, she heard the inmates rather than saw them at this time of day. Shouts from one room, hoarse cackling from another.

It was a prison. She dressed in a dull grey uniform and was shown to a roomful of women who were preparing for bed in a long dormitory. Nobody took any notice of her. She was too sick of heart to speak in any case. She lay down and cried bitterly into her hard pillow. She was tempted to feel there was no hope now. Her mother, father and brothers were lost to her, for she had not much expectation that Pip would return for her as soon as he thought. That he was a fond, loyal brother she had no doubt of, but how long would it take him to earn enough to find rent for even one small room? London was a huge disappointment for her.

Neither she nor her brother had had any idea that it would be difficult to find a situation in London. She thought she would have unpacked her bundle in a servant's attic room—bad as they were, they were in secure family homes. She thought she would have been absorbed into a household with other servants, given food and promised a wage, and become friends with the other staff there.

She and Pip ought to have tried harder before giving up. No, they ought to have looked for situations before they had left Whitholm. They had been impatient to be gone, unable to withstand another day with Henry and his unfeeling in-laws. And they had tumbled unprepared into a harsh, unfeeling world.

They should have returned to Hetherton. It would not have been as bad as this! But it was too late now for such thoughts. She had one thought in her head—the thought that had made her agree to Pip's plan—she would stay here long enough to rest and fill her stomach, and then she would slip away. But leave to what? She kept returning to the same dilemma.

The following morning, she was put to work in the infirmary laundry and spent the day washing soiled linen and turning the mangle. It was dirty, heavy work, and the smells were very unpleasant. She turned her mind and body to it mechanically, feeling numb. She kept a sullen silence. The food was plain but nourishing after her days of hunger.

I have to get out, she kept saying to herself. *There must be a way! I have to get out!*

She tried to speak with the Matron who did her rounds daily, but she was not interested in hearing of yet another inmate's problems.

"Everybody has troubles here," she said dismissively.

"Please can you find me a situation outside?"

"A situation? If you were a bit young, twelve or thirteen, I could find you a place as a kitchen maid, but at your age employers think your character is formed and it mightn't be to their liking."

This was Matron's explanation. In truth she was a very lazy woman who supplied young, cheap labour to her friends. The older, stronger girls were useful to her for the back-breaking female jobs occupations in the workhouse —the kitchen, the laundry.

Matron told her that she could leave whenever she wanted with forty-eight hours' notice, but Babs knew that without a situation to go to, this would be a very unwise thing to do. She would have to bide her time.

ESCAPE

She did not see Pip for two weeks, and when she did, she saw how thin he had become. But he was pleased at her appearance.

"You're not starving," he said.

"No, I'm not—though the food is not at all nice—but I'm thankful for it. What of you? Do you have a job?"

"Not a regular job. I go to the docks and when the foreman comes out looking for day labourers, I jostle forward so he'll see me—I am lucky sometimes. But I have made friends, and they look out for me. If they get taken on, I do too; and if I get taken on, I ask for them."

"Where do you live?"

"A lodging house. A doss house, they call it. It isn't much." Pip did not elaborate. By his appearance, Babs knew he was only just getting by and that his chance of making a life for himself and for her was narrow. Pip visited her every two weeks and life did not seem to be getting any better for him. She took to saving him some bread which he gladly accepted and ate right away.

In April, Matron called her from the laundry to come to her small, dark office.

"Do you still want a situation outside?" she asked her.

"Yes, yes I do!" Babs held her breath until Matron spoke again.

"I've seen how you work in the laundry—you have experience of that now. Very valuable experience. There's a cousin of mine with a laundry, he needs a girl."

"Yes, I accept!"

"His name is Mr. Frank Norris and this is his address." She passed a piece of paper to her. "You'll get your own clothes back and belongings when you leave here. When will you go?"

"As soon as I can!" Bets said, exulting in her great fortune, for so it seemed to her at the time. "But Matron, where shall I live?"

"There's a dormitory you will share with the other girls."

Fed and found! Babs was elated. She clutched the address to her and asked Matron to please give it also to her brother Pip when he arrived to see her. She promised that she would. Her heart sang as she left two days later for Shoreditch where Mr. Norris ran his laundry.

THE LAUNDRY

Her employer was a wiry man with eyes close together and a long nose. He reminded Babs of a fox.

"You give any trouble, you're out," he said to her, his thumbs in his belt.

"I won't give any trouble, sir."

"Good. Glad to 'ear it. Follow orders." She did not like the way he looked her up and down.

The other 'girls' were hardly that; they were middle-aged women who shouted and laughed a great deal at anything at all.

The laundry and living quarters were all at ground level, the dormitory tucked behind the laundry.

"Here, you take the bed nearest the window," said the bossy one, laughing.

The other women chuckled. Babs wondered why. The window looked out on the alley. The curtains were thin. As they prepared for bed, she tried to stay out of sight of it. But Mr. Norris passed the window, looking in.

The women burst into loud laughter. Babs did not think it at all amusing.

It soon became apparent to Babs that she was the object of his attention. He stood too close to her when she was at the machines, he came behind her and squeezed her waist and pinched her arm, all to the bawdy laughter of the other women. She was upset that they found this entertaining.

When it came to giving her week's wages, he told her that he did not bring hers.

"Come to my rooms," he said. "I will 'ave it there, and if you're a good girl, some extra."

The other women exploded in raucous laughter.

Babs flushed red.

"I'd prefer to receive my wages here," she said.

"But I do not have it 'ere," he said, smiling, and glancing in amusement at the other women.

"How come I'm not invited to your rooms for my mint," roared Bertha in merriment.

The banter continued in a vulgar way. Babs knew she was being made fun of.

"I was only joking, Miss Serious Face," said Mr. Norris. "Here you are, your shillings, less sixpence for trailing the end of the tablecloth on the floor and it having to be washed again. Be more careful next week."

Babs knew she could not stay in this place. She had her week's wages; she left the following morning before anybody was up.

She had had an idea of how to keep herself—could she use her own God-given gifts? She could sing. But first she had to try to find Pip. The docklands could not be very far off. All she had to do was ask for directions to the River Thames and she was sure she would be almost there.

It was farther than she thought. And her search was fruitless. So many docks and wharves spreading out over miles! She stopped and asked several men if they knew a Philip or Pip Wren, but it was futile, and some of the men thought she was approaching them for company and were reluctant to let her go. Nobody had heard of him, and she felt afraid in this rough area full of shady-looking characters some of whom were staring at a woman walking alone, looking about her. There were women at street corners calling endearments out to the men, and a few of them called angrily to her, telling her to 'ger out!'

and 'go somewhere else!' She felt humiliated and an oddity in an area such as this.

I don't wish to bide here, she thought, and began a long walk whence she came, but she got lost and ended up in an area named Hackney. Though the streets looked shabby and poor, she saw families and felt safer there. She decided to stay. She went to a second-hand shop and purchased an old straw hat without holes in it and a colourful shawl that had seen better days.

STREET SINGER

Babs was able to afford lodging that night and the following morning she chose a busy corner and wrapped her bright shawl about her. At least she would be seen, and hopefully heard! The cheap hat was at her feet. She began to sing. At first her voice quavered—her voice sounded so alien among the varied sounds of the street traffic, but as passersby began to throw pennies into the cap, it grew stronger. The pile of pennies grew bigger and for the first time since she had come to London, she felt hopeful.

There were a few urchins hanging about, their eyes on the pile of copper pennies accumulating in her hat. They looked hungry and edged closer. The poor little things had thin limbs and were barefoot in the cold, dirty street. Their eyes, large in their faces, held her and she stopped and gave them some pennies to go and buy bread.

After that, they returned fortified and the biggest and oldest of them, a lad about twelve, stood in the middle of the path instructing the public to 'give to the singin' lady' in tones rather more threatening than appealing, so that they hurried by, frowning.

"Billy," she said to him. "It's very nice of you to try to increase my business. But I think you should go on your way now."

He looked at the pile of coppers and she sighed and gave him some more and the others too. They ran off, whooping with joy.

She stopped for a while to rest her voice and went into a nearby bar for a drink of water. She had been afraid to go in until she saw some women enter and that gave her courage. She was further reassured to see that there was a woman behind the bar.

She stayed in that spot and made herself a steady, if small sum. She sang in all weathers and went into the pub—the Lionheart—for water and tea. She played her mouth organ when she was tired of singing. She found a cheap place to sleep. She was earning just enough to keep herself, and there was a flower market where she had plenty of customers.

She tried out different spots in the area to see what yielded the best tips, and she learned that the closer she was to a public house the better, for a man a little drunk was more likely to flip a few pennies—even a threepenny bit or a sixpence—into her hat. She did not like drunken men—they were either generous or amorous, but she learned to deal with the latter with humour which was a great deal better than making them angry. She had several propositions to go with them to unknown destinations where they would be sure to have a good time, and a drunken proposal of marriage at least once a week.

On her walks in the city, she always looked for Swanns Furniture, and was sorry more than once for not asking Caleb or Alice where in London it was. If she knew, she'd pay Caleb a call. But she thought that Caleb would be shocked to see her so bedraggled and thin.

The summer made the streets smell badly, but business was fair. She sang her way through it, and autumn came in, bringing with it cold but a welcome reprieve from the dreadful smells, but now the air was thick with fog and soot, making singing more difficult as she developed a cough.

One Sunday she made her way back to Brownton workhouse and asked if her brother had been to see her and if he had left any message. But Matron was gone, and the new woman knew nothing about her. She grew despondent. If only she had paper and pen, she could try writing to Henry to find out if he knew anything, but she had not, nor could she afford a writing pad and a pen.

When she returned from her long walk, it was to find out that she had been robbed of her small savings that she had thought she had hidden safely. The landlady and the other tenants said they knew nothing about it, and the landlady did nothing about finding it. Knowing she could not trust any of them, she moved to another lodging house, a cheaper, dirtier and worse one. She knew she could hardly afford to eat now, and she became ill on and off.

DARK DECEMBER

B abs applied to music and dance halls for employment. But it never came to anything, for the kind of music in demand was not what Aunt Kitty had taught her, and she had no instrument upon which she could learn new pieces or practice. Her demonstrations ended in the potential employer stopping her and thanking her and saying that they needed somebody who could play modern, popular songs and dance pieces.

She also had the idea of teaching piano, but that was no good either without a proper room and an instrument, and she needed to look more respectable if she were to gain admittance to a family home to teach children. Her clothes were almost rags now, an old green striped gown patched so much the original was hardly visible, and there was a new rent every day; her shawl dulled with threads pulled and her thin cloak the worse for wear, her straw bonnet drab and shapeless, the yellow ribbons and artificial flowers limp and ragged. Her boots let in water and her feet were chilled all the time.

"Why don't you make some on the side like we do?" asked a girl at her lodgings as she sat on her mattress and combed out her long red hair. "You won't like it at first, but you'll get used to it. We don't starve and we get enough to buy warm clothing and suchlike."

"I'm not starving, Nora." Babs was filing her nails. She liked to have shapely nails. That was one thing about not working as a servant; that would ruin them. But she was hungry a lot of the time.

"Well, if you ever are interested, come to me. Some part-time work to fill the gaps. There's one woman I know, a governess, who was thrown out of her situation on account of the master liking her too much; she couldn't get another, so that's what she does now. She goes with men. If she didn't, she'd starve."

This was a shocking story and Babs decided if a governess could not get a post without a reference, what chance did she have? But she would never resort to prostitution to keep herself from starving. The workhouse was better than that. To think that a governess could be reduced to working the streets! It was a cruel world.

For the moment then, singing alone would have to sustain her for the bare necessities of life. At least with Christmas coming, she could sing all the carols she knew, and people would be generous. She was confident of earning more in December, and she hoped it would be enough to give herself a shorter time out-of-doors in the chilly January days.

But disaster struck her just two weeks before Christmas. She was singing near a bakehouse at Martello Street. It was a favourite place of hers because of the aromas and the popularity of the baker, and at the end of the business day she could buy a day-old bun for a penny. This had been her main meal for weeks now.

It was a dull, cold day. Late in the afternoon the sky darkened ominously, and it began to pour chilly rain in a steady downpour. Usually when it rained, she took shelter as best she could until it stopped; but today the shopfront where she usually went had a gate across it because of a family bereavement. The baker had sold out early and was closed. By the time she found another shopfront, she was soaked through. The rain persisted; she did not have enough for her rent, and she had to begin singing again. As soon as she had enough for rent and food, she gathered up her hat and went home to her damp lodging house.

She took off her wet things and set them out to dry and got into her nightdress. She lay down on the straw mattress, her body's aching eased for the moment. She felt hot and then shivered with cold. This continued for a day and she got no better. Her voice was only a croak.

"You're sick, Babs," said Nora. "Have you got any money for medicine? Give it here; I'll go to the chemist."

But on her way to the chemist Nora passed the Brown Foxe and went in for one, just one. She was cold and she was sure that Babs would not grudge her one to warm her up. She met friends there to whom she owed money, and they demanded payment, so she used Babs's paltry sum to placate them.

She returned to the lodging house to find that Babs was worse. She told a lie about the medicine.

"He hasn't any, luv. So many people are down with this influenza, he's out of it and so is every other chemist."

Babs was too sick to ask for her money back. Nora made her hot tea.

"I have to get better! I have to or Mrs. Bridges will throw me out!"

CRISIS ON CHRISTMAS EVE

The landlady had no mercy on defaulters. She ran a tight ship and any woman who did not have the rent on Friday was ejected on Saturday.

Nora felt dreadfully guilty, and so she had a whip-around for the rent and paid it.

"What about that medicine, Nora? Can you try again?" Babs asked her.

"It's an epidemic and there's no medicine," Nora repeated the lie.

"It can't be true," Babs lamented, but she was too weak to even think beyond this.

Mrs. Bridges came to her bedside and inspected her.

"You have to go, Babs. You'll infect everyone here if you stay, and all the girls will be sick. This here isn't a 'ospital. Not a charity neither. Get up and go to the 'ospital where you'll be looked arter. Polly, Jane, get 'er up and dressed and take 'er to the 'ospital first thing tomorrow mornin'."

"But it's Christmas Eve!" they objected. They had a busy day ahead; there would be revellers a-plenty roaming around the streets looking for girls. They might earn enough money to buy a bit of finery for the Season.

"You can't take a sick woman to the 'ospital? Where's your Christmas spirit?" Mrs. Bridges asked them belligerently.

"Where's yours?" Jane asked. "Look at 'er there, burnin' with fever, and you would throw 'er out Christmas Eve."

"There are doctors at the 'ospital," Mrs. Bridges said with a little sarcasm. "Do you think she'll live without a doctor? I say she won't. I give 'er two days more and she'll ring in the New Year in the churchyard."

At that, the girls agreed to take her to the hospital. The following morning, they got her up and dressed and hailed a cart. The carter demanded a shilling, and they thought it too much.

"Jane, the workhouse is nearer than the 'ospital. Why don't we take 'er there? There's a doctor in the workhouse, isn't there? She'll be looked arter as good as anywhere else. How much to the workhouse?"

"Ninepence," he said.

"Away with your ninepence! Not a penny more 'n fourpence!" Jane said.

They agreed on sixpence.

When Babs realised that she was being taken to a workhouse, she roused herself sufficiently to object.

"No, I'm not going to the workhouse," she said.

"We haven't time to take you to the 'ospital," Jane said. "So we're taking you to the workhouse. There's an 'orspital there, what's the difference?"

"Let me be!" Babs raised herself sufficiently to shake off her companions. "Go away! I won't go to any workhouse! I was there once and I'm never going back!"

The women looked at one another; the carter got his old horse moving again and he shuffled up the street.

"Now look, he's gone an' all."

"Go away!" Babs was delirious. "I'll manage by myself—"

Her companions shrugged and decided to leave her to herself.

"We done our best, we did." They said to each other.

THE RESCUER

Bets leaned against a lamp post for support and looked about her. Her head swam and her heart pounded. She coughed. She felt very ill indeed but she had to get herself to Hackney Hospital before she got any worse.

She walked down the street and turned the corner and then another. The busy district was filling up with last-minute shoppers, the men in greatcoats and mufflers around their throats; the women clad in warm wool coats and furs. There was an air of anticipation as there always is on Christmas Eve, an air of hurry, of cheer, of impending joy. But she felt no joy today.

She stopped someone to ask directions to the hospital, and immediately forgot them, as she was so ill. The groceryman who directed her seemed to be a little unreal as he turned and pointed and made signs for left and right—she nodded over and over but she had lost him almost immediately he began his instructions. She trudged on, her feet cold in her boots, her entire body shivering with fever. She was on a street by a canal. Her head grew so hot she pushed back her bonnet and the frayed ribbons loosened. It slipped from her head and her hair, which had been caught up in a bun, tumbled down about her shoulders. The bonnet was picked up a few minutes later by a few children who threw it to one another, running as they went toward the canal. There, it went into the water, so they forgot about it and ran off.

She was in a strange area now but it hardly mattered—she simply put one foot in front of another and left the canal road to get onto a proper street. She was vaguely aware of carol singers somewhere, everything was merry and bright somewhere, somewhere far away. Lights began to shine as dusk came on early. Lamps on carriages, twinkling lights in shop windows. Children laughed in delight, and outside a bakery a family of little ones chimed for gingerbread. She was vaguely aware of the children. She heard their chirping voices and then: "Come away, children, don't look. Don't look." She was barely aware that she was what they were looking at. Did she look so dreadful that adults turned their children away from her?

She trudged on. She was lost now.

She began to feel that she would never get to any hospital

because she would have to lie down on the way. She swayed, and a woman looked at her in disgust.

"Drunk at this time of day—and hatless! Disgraceful!" she said to her companion.

"Christmas means nothing to some people!" was the reply. It took Babs a moment to realise that they were speaking of her.

A few streets later she felt she could go no further. She was walking by a shop that had tables and chairs in the window. There was a covered porch in front of the big handsome main door.

I will lie down for a little. She thought and lowered herself onto the ground. She was aware of people coming and going from the shop and of their remarks.

"Look at her, George. Drunk!"

"This street used to be respectable once. It's gone down."

"Why do the police not come and take those dirty lazy beggars out of our sight!"

Dirty lazy beggar. Is that what she looked like? Her breath became short, and she shut her eyes.

I am dying, she thought. *I will die here—oh Mama, Papa, when you come back, you will find out I have died, but I can't help myself—I'm too far gone now...Jesus, my Lord and Saviour.* She felt herself sink toward the ground and murmured prayers. The world was becoming farther away.

"Excuse me, can you get this beggar removed from here?" a female upper-class voice sounded annoyed. "I almost had to step over her."

"I will get someone from the shop," said another voice. A few moments later Babs was conscious of someone bending over her.

"Please get that beggar away from here," snipped the same upper-class voice.

"I don't see 'er begging," said a kind male voice. It came from the person bending over her.

"Impertinent! Well, Mister, I do not wish to patronise your establishment if you have this filth lying in front of it. A wanton, bareheaded woman."

"A Merry Christmas to you, then, Madam." said the male voice again with a dismissive intonation.

"Who do you think you are to speak to me like that? I will see to it, boy, that you are dismissed! I am going to speak to Mr. Swann."

"This young woman is ill, Lady Chappleton. She's burning up with fever. Mr. Swann will be back on the 28th, if you wish to speak with him about me, and my name is Caleb Dalton. Now I have to get this poor creature to a hospital."

Caleb Dalton!

The woman's voice changed—it seemed that the young

man was putting her to shame. "I'm sorry," she stammered. "You are correct—she is very ill."

"She needs to go to a hospital. Be so good as to ask your coachman to call a cab, Lady Chappleton, please?"

ST BARTHOLOMEW'S

Caleb! Oh Caleb! It's you, and you do not know me, because I am so altered! I am thin and ill! My appearance must be so changed! I pray you do not recognise me, in my present state!

Babs then felt herself swept off the cold ground and into a pair of strong arms. Her head was against his greatcoat. She kept her eyes shut tightly.

"The poor girl weighs less than a feather," she heard him say. "Where is the nearest hospital?" he called out to somebody.

"Barts in Smithfield," a male voice answered, and she felt herself lifted into a carriage and laid upon the seat. Her hand clutched his lapel—she was afraid to let him go.

"She's conscious," she heard Caleb say. "Don't worry, Miss, I won't leave you until you are safely at the hospital."

His voice brought such comfort, such balm to her heart that a tear escaped down her hot, grimy cheek. She felt it wiped away.

"Hurry up, man!" she heard Caleb shout.

The carriage began to move at a rapid pace. Tears coursed down her cheeks but still she kept her eyes shut—terrified of being recognised as the healthy, happy girl Caleb had known before. He continued to wipe her tears away with his handkerchief and reassured her that she was not to fret. His voice reassured her more than his words—his accent, so dear and familiar.

The carriage came to a halt again and she was lifted out and again carried in his arms inside a building—she heard him speak to the porter, then to a nurse, and finally she was laid gently upon a bed.

"We will take over now, sir." A nurse said.

"I must go," he said. "I have to catch a train. Miss—are you able to speak? I should love to know your name, Miss."

She kept her eyes shut and did not respond, but he detected a little twitch of her mouth. She could hear him.

"Please look after her well," she heard him say. "I'm going into Essex now, but I'll return in three days and I hope I find her well. No, I know nothing of her. I found her lying outside my place of employment."

"I can tell you she's malnourished, and maybe tubercular," said a nurse.

"As bad as that! I hope not! Maybe with some good food —" his voice trailed away as he left.

They were busy about her then—she was washed, and put into fresh clothes, and the doctor came with his jar of leeches and bled her. She fell asleep, and when she awoke in the dark later, she wondered if she had imagined it all.

But no, Caleb Dalton had saved her life.

In Hackney, the girls were not having much success attracting custom that Christmas Eve. Jane and Polly's consciences made them quiet and sullen as they sipped gin at the King Henry tavern.

"We shouldn't have left 'er," said Polly suddenly. "She might fall over on 'er way. I'm going out to look for 'er."

"I'll come with you," Jane jumped up to join her. "I'll not 'ave it on my conscience neither."

They remembered that she had trudged up a long street and luckily, a shopkeeper remembered her and pointed them in the direction she had taken. This brought them to the road by the canal, and there floating upon the water, caught in some stones near the bank they saw a familiar bonnet, its yellow ribbons and decorations identifying it as one they knew.

"It couldn't be! Oh Polly! I'm that afeard to look!"

"It's 'ers, Jane. It's Babs's bonnet. I know it."

"Oh Polly—is she—did she—?"

"She went in, Jane. She must've."

"Oh did she fall? Or was it deliberate?" Polly took her head in her hands.

"We 'ave to tell the police."

They hurried to tell a constable, who said he would look into it. Then they hurried home, heavy in heart. It was a Christmas Eve they would rather forget.

The police were not alarmed however when another constable coming in from his beat said that he had seen a hatless woman walking along that way a few hours before, it was most likely hers. She was drunk but not causing any trouble, so he had let her pass by. It was a relief; nobody had seen anybody go into the canal and nobody wanted the task of looking for a body on Christmas Eve. It was time to go home and enjoy the festivities.

DALTON'S CHRISTMAS

Caleb could not get the girl out of his mind as the train sped toward Chelmsford. A little frail creature, pretty in appearance, even in illness. How had she come to this awful situation? Had she been born into poverty? Her fingers were long and soft and her nails clean and nicely shaped. She was not a servant then, nor did she live by manual labour. Her clothes were very poor. She lived by some other means other than manual work. She was not surely a—a prostitute? He doubted it very much, for those ladies wore showy garments and trinkets. Poor but showy—the shawl was colourful though—he really did not know what to think about the girl whose life he had saved. Several scenarios played themselves out in his mind as he travelled, and none of them satisfied him as to her background.

As usual he was greeted with delight at home in the same little cottage he'd grown up in. Though he was now a favoured employee of Mr. Swann, the family was relieved to find that he was still the same Caleb, except that his manner of speech had altered a little—he no longer had as broad a country accent as before and he pronounced certain words differently.

Alice was living at home once again. Her mother had broken her arm in the summer, and she had left service. Caleb's regular presents of money had enabled the family to keep her at home. For Christmas he had brought sweets and cakes and a pair of kid gloves for his mother and a felt hat for his father; Alice was the recipient of three spools of fancy laces.

"Who 'elped you to choose them?" Alice said in delight. "I don't for a moment think you chose them yourself! This one for my bonnet, it will give it a new life, won't it, Ma?"

"Miss Swann picked them out. She's very helpful in matters like these," he said. "She wished to know the colour of your hair and eyes and I was 'ard put to remember!"

"They're the same as yours, you silly. Miss Swann? She takes such an interest?" Alice smiled with mischief as her brother coloured and made her a smart answer.

Though he chatted with them, they felt his mind was elsewhere.

"Is it Miss Swann who's on your mind?" his mother asked, a teasing smile on her face. "It would not be a bad thing; her father was of a 'umble background, I heard, his mother a milliner from Colchester, they would make no objection!"

"Oh Ma, please don't tease me so. I'm not thinking of Miss Swann."

Something else was said, and then Caleb added:

"I must tell you an odd thing that happened to me just as I left work today." They listened intently as he recounted the episode in detail.

"That be a very good deed, a very kind service for a poor misfortunate girl," his father said, puffing his pipe.

"And she be ill as that? Not just the worse for wear, for gin?" his mother asked.

"No, Ma. She was not drunk. She was burning with fever. I'm afraid she might not live—they said perhaps consumption."

"Consumption!" A cloud came over his mother's countenance. "I 'ope she did not infect you!"

"Ma, don't fret like that. I was only in her company a half-hour. When I return, I'll visit her and I'll write to tell you as 'ow she is."

"There be no need for that, Caleb, and no need to visit 'er," his mother said with spirit. "How do you know anything about 'er? If she recovers, she'll give them 'er name and no doubt somebody will claim 'er. But I'm glad you took it upon yourself to do something, when everybody else was passin' her by, especially at Christmas. But there be no need for you to do anymore."

"Is there any news of the Wrens?" he asked then to change the subject.

"No, not since Mr. Henry came to take Pip and Babs to his home at Whitholm, and you know about that. We 'aven't seen them since."

"I saw Pip in London," Caleb said then, but a frown furrowed his brow. "We do business with a warehouse near Victoria Docks, and I was on my way there once about an order for office furniture, and it just 'appened to be when the labourers were being discharged for the day. They were surging out of the dock gates, about one hundred men. I heard someone call: "Pip Wren!" and wheeled around to see who it was, and my eyes followed the man who'd shouted—I saw Pip turn about. *That's never our Pip, I thought, for he's very thin.* He it was. He was one of the labourers. He did not see me. The following day I made it my business to be there again, and this time I saw him clearly, coming out with the other men. I went up to him."

"Did he know you?" Alice asked eagerly.

"Yes, he did. He said: '*Chippy—Chippy Dalton*—but he seemed embarrassed; not too pleased to see me, not at first, but then he was very friendly."

"What 'appened? What did he say?"

"I said: 'I thought you were at your brother's house,' and he said that he left there because he didn't see eye to eye with him. So he came to London, but a position he sought did not turn out as expected, so he was living in Stepney and doing labouring work until he found a better job."

"Did you ask him about Babs?" Alice asked him eagerly.

"I did—he said he had not heard from 'er for a while. But he did not wish to be delayed, and I let 'im go. I told him he should go back to Hetherton, where he'd get steady work on the farms come spring. He said 'e might, but it depended on how his affairs went in London. I felt sorry for 'im. Somethin's not right, it's not."

"I do 'ope Pip comes back, come spring," Alice said. "I always liked Pip."

"What of the Wren parents? Any news?" Caleb asked.

"No, not a thing. They be almost certainly dead," his mother said. "Come on, it's late. Let's all of us go to bed. Up early tomorrow for church and to put the bird in."

"Where did you get the bird?"

"The new people up at Redgate. A nice family, they are."

Three days later Alice walked with her brother back to the railway station.

"Don't take on now, Caleb, but Mama and Papa, they want me to say somethin' to you."

"And what be that?" Caleb asked, a little crossly.

"They said—and remember I'm only the messenger, they said—*tell Caleb not to throw himself away.*"

Caleb made an impatient sigh but said nothing.

"You not be cross with me, I hope," Alice said.

"Oh no, not cross with you at all," he said. "You've done your duty now, so rest easy."

RECOVERING

~~~

In London, Caleb went straight from the railway station to St Bartholomew's Hospital and made his way to the women's ward. He felt a happy anticipation tempered by a horrid dread—was she alive or dead? When he got there, he was relieved to see her delicate, pale face upon the pillow, her dark hair peeping out of her white cap, but she was sleeping.

"How is she?" he asked the nurse.

"Improving a little. Her fever has come down."

"Did she tell you her name?"

"Anne White, and that is all we know about her."

Babs heard his voice and kept her eyes closed. She did not wish him to know her. He came to her bedside; she knew he was there. A tender hand was placed on her head.

"I'm prayin' for you, Miss White." was all he said. Her heart almost burst with feeling—she contained herself with difficulty.

Caleb returned twice more, and each time Miss White was sleeping. But her condition had improved. The deathly whiteness of her complexion had gone; she had a little colour, and her delicate features did not look as gaunt as before.

She reminds me of someone, Caleb thought.

"Has anybody claimed her?" He asked the nurses.

"No, nobody at all. But we can tell she is respectable, if you know what I mean, sir. We have our regulars and know them, they often come to us, having had some accident or other while in gin, or a man rough them up, but this girl, we haven't seen before. We think that she got into that bad state because she had no occupation and wouldn't go on the streets like many have to do, to keep herself from starving. The good news, sir, is that the doctor doesn't think she has tuberculosis, because her lungs are not inflamed and her cough has eased."

"I'm that happy to hear it! What will she do when she leaves?"

"If she has nowhere to go, it'll be the workhouse."

"Oh no, not there!" Caleb's reaction was one of horror. "Here, I want to give you some money for her. I have to go into Sussex with my employer in a few days; if you'd be so good as to give her this." He produced two sovereigns. "It's not much but it might help her. I'll be back in a week's time."

Babs had been given some medicine that made her sleepy and did not overhear this conversation, so she was a little disappointed to hear that her 'saviour' as the nurses called Mr. Dalton, had been in but then surprised and very emotional that he had left her some money to give her a start when she left. She thought a great deal about what to do with it, how best it would serve her.

What can I do? Singing on street corners is all very well until it rains, so I can't depend on that. I can read, I can write, I have a little education, could I teach? I will need some new clothes. I will need a room, or lodging. I must be very sparing with this until I get on my feet. I wish I could find Pip! Where is my brother?

A NEW BEGINNING

The nurses had grown fond of their young charge, and when they told her that she was discharged, she took the opportunity of asking the Ward Sister for a 'character' to set her on her way. She said she could not do so, but asked the chaplain, who on her recommendation wrote that Miss White was of good character, cheerful and honest. It was more valuable to have one from a clergyman.

The nurse came with her clothes, her awful green striped gown and her ragged shawl and threadbare mantle. "You came without a hat," they said to her. "But we have one belonging to someone who died, their relations didn't want it, it's a bit old-fashioned."

It was a horrid brown straw hat with no trimming whatsoever. However, 'beggars can't be choosers' so she put it on.

She put her hand in her mantle pockets.

"My mouth organ! It's gone! Have you seen it?"

The nurses itemised patients' belongings upon admission, but no mouth organ was on the list.

"It could have fallen out of your pocket when Mr. Dalton brought you here," they said to her. "You were in his arms…"

The mouth organ that Caleb had made was gone. It was a further upset, for all her links to her childhood in Hetherton had disappeared.

"Never mind, Anne. You're going to make a new life for yourself, and go to the Women's Refuge in Holborn. Don't look back, look forward."

This was the advice of the nurse and she decided to take it to heart as best she could as she pulled on her boots, hard and pinched.

The Women's Refuge was a charitable enterprise by a few ladies who were concerned that young women in London were falling into prostitution because of necessity, and they admitted her there. She shared a room with three other girls and immediately felt at home. Nearly all of the girls in the Refuge were from the country and all had found London very bewildering and dangerous. Some had been lured by false promises of work, only to find themselves working as prostitutes. They would stay until they found live-in situations in family homes or until somebody from their village came to bring them home.

If only I could find Pip! She thought of him very often and felt tormented. *Did Matron of the workhouse give him my address? But then I left there so suddenly, that even if he had found the Laundry, nobody knew where I went from there. How do I find my brother?*

Caleb was constantly on her mind. She longed to see him again, but she had to build herself up and become more like the healthy girl he knew in Hetherton. She cherished the memory of his attention and care of her. On that Christmas Eve when she was very ill and wandered about the London streets, she had not taken note of where Swanns Furniture was—she had not even known it was there until Caleb appeared—but she knew she was in or near Smithfield, and she was determined to find it. For she planned to see him again as soon as she was well, to thank him. In the meantime, she was busy responding to advertisements that the charitable Ladies put in front of her.

"Here is a woman in Holborn needing a parlourmaid," said one, putting a newspaper clipping in front of her. "She is known to me, a good woman."

A week later, Babs was in the Holborn home and settled in with the other servants. She felt happy because this is what she had intended to do when she had come to London. But it was harder than she had thought! She had to rise very early in the chill of the morning and light fires in all the rooms, including the bedrooms. The housekeeper was strict. The butler was imposing and snooty. She was dismayed at how little time off she was allowed. One half-day per month! She thought of the servants at Redgate, she'd never known how hard it was for them!

How could she find Pip? How could she make her own clothes to improve her wardrobe so that she could move on to something better? And oh dear, her nails! Short and broken, she was not happy at all with the way they looked!

But she was too busy eating the healthy food put in front of her, too busy with her work, too busy making herself a few nice items to wear to notice the time passing, and soon it was summer.

HARVEY VERNON

Caleb was a firm favourite with Mr. Swann, and it did not escape the employer that his own daughter was sweet on his apprentice. He heartily approved, although his wife was sceptical.

"Stella's friends would not give Caleb the time of day," she pointed out to her husband one evening.

"That's to their loss, then." He retorted. "I think it would be a fine thing to have a son-in-law like Caleb Dalton. He's cut from my own cloth, so to speak. Of humble origins, gifted, hardworking. I see a lot of myself in him."

"Stella does like him," Mrs. Swann said. "But to go so low, dear! Are you sure you're not trying to poke your business associates in the eye? I know you."

Mr. Swann was contemptuous of what he called the New Rich, who as soon as they got a fat bank account, forgot where they had come from and scorned former friends and acquaintances. It would delight him to tell them that his daughter was to marry the son of a shepherd.

"Go so low, you say? Not any lower than you went, Mrs. Swann."

"Oh, come now, you did not come from a shepherd's cottage, as he does."

"No, but it was not much better. My father was a labourer and my mother a milliner. She it was that pushed me into cabinet-making."

"I remember her well," said Mrs. Swann, a little ironically. The old Mrs. Swann had been a force to be reckoned with. She was intelligent, wore beautiful hats, and had driven her son hard to make something of himself. She had added an extra 'n' to their original surname Swan. She had approved the match with Miss Mary Vernon, whose family's wealth was from investments in the West Indies.

"I suggest Caleb dine with us in future," said Mr. Swann. "Not just Sundays. Every meal, every day. He's far above a servant in this house. And he needs a room of his own. Give him the butler's room." The Swanns did not keep a butler; Mr. Swann thought that most people had them for show. The butler's room was empty.

"Thomas?" Her voice was tense in enquiry, and he braced himself for what was coming.

"What is it?" he asked sharply.

"What about Harvey?"

Harvey was the son of Mrs. Swann's deceased brother who they had adopted a few years before. Harvey was idle, dilettante, and expected to inherit the business.

Mr. Swann did not reply, so his wife repeated the question.

"I don't know about Harvey." The terse reply took her off guard.

"Thomas," she said, "Harvey could well feel you may be edging him out."

"Harvey has no interest in work," was her husband's reply. "He won't get his lily-white hands smudged with oil or covered in sawdust."

This troubled Mrs. Swann.

"You must give him a chance, Thomas!"

"Mary, must we speak of this again? I have given that lad every chance. He won't learn the business."

"He does not have to know the craft," Mrs. Swann countered. "He can be a manager. He can run it from the top."

"I won't have him involved in the business if he doesn't learn woodcraft, and that's final." Mr. Swann got up and paced the room. His face became red with anger. "I have no patience with men who direct operations they know nothing about."

"What is he to do, Thomas?" His wife's tone was cold.

"He can choose a profession. I will send him to Oxford or Cambridge or wherever he wants. Law or something. But he won't be coming into the business. I have chosen my —successor."

Mrs. Swann looked intently at him.

"If Stella does not marry him, what then?"

"Stella will marry him! She loves him! It's obvious, the sheep's eyes she makes at him."

"She could well grow out of it and meet another young man and there, your plan is gone up in flames." Mrs. Swann was a little angry now.

"Let us leave the subject, woman," he said, redder than ever with rage.

They settled into an uncomfortable silence.

"And Caleb will eat with us." Mr. Swann said firmly.

AN OLD SHEPHERD'S ADVICE

So it happened that Caleb took his seat at the table of Mrs Swann, and had Stella seated opposite him at every sitting. She was a tall, slim girl, fair-skinned with brown hair and pale blue eyes. She liked the new addition very much. Seated beside her was her cousin Harvey Vernon, who looked with contempt at Caleb, and took every opportunity to put him down. He laughed at his accent, his odd pronunciation, repeating them to himself. He left Caleb in no doubt as to how he felt about his presence there.

The situation troubled the shepherd's son. When he was at home in the summer, he went to his father in the field and, hoping to get advice, told him all.

"So ye think this lad be thinkin' that you're about to take 'is place," Alf said.

"Yes, and—"

"And—are you? Takin' his place?"

"I think Mr. Swann favours me, yes."

"Has the girl anything got to do with'n?"

"Yes, I think she has. She likes me. And—her father has dropped hints to me. Strong hints."

"And do you like her?"

"Well, yes, I suppose I do..."

"You're not convincin' me, Caleb."

"I could be happy with her, I suppose, she's a nice girl."

"Is there any another girl?"

Caleb shifted uncomfortably.

"No, no. I don't know any other girl I like."

"Your mother was afeard of that girl you brought to the 'ospital. You seemed very taken with her, and were in another world all the time you were 'ere."

"I don't know where she is, Father, or what became of her."

His father was silent for a time.

"If this young relative don't like you, and resents you, will it be worth 'n? You don't seem to love Miss Swann, and if she 'n her father weren't pushin' theirselves at you, you mightn't think of her at all. Tha's my opinion."

"You know, Father, I always thought I wanted to strike out on my own when I was a Master Cabinet Maker. Come back here to Hetherton and open a business. Or Chelmsford maybe. London doesn't attract me. My apprenticeship will be over soon. I'll have to make up my mind, for if I stay on beyond next year..."

"...you will have an understanding with Miss Swann and a proposal will be expected. Don't do anything until you have that Master's certificate in your fist. But—one thing—like should marry like. Either you become one of them, or she become like us."

"Thanks for the advice, Father."

To change the subject, Caleb asked if his father had seen any sign of Pip Wren.

"No, he din't come back, not to these parts anyway."

PIP'S TROUBLE

Pip stuck his feet under a standpipe on the street while his friend pumped cold water onto them. It was a hot summer and London was sweltering in a heat wave.

"I don't know which is worse, bitter cold and soot in winter, or summer with its boiling pavements and its stink," he said to his friend Mike.

"London is always sweet to me," Mike replied. He had been born in London. "I went out the country once, Pip, I couldn't stick it, the cows mooing was the only sound, an' sheep's bells. Not a shop for miles where I could get a bite to eat. How anybody sticks the country I don't know."

Pip laughed and then Pip pumped for his friend, then for a dog who approached hopefully and went under the stream of water, his tongue out to catch some to drink before he finished. "You could've asked at a farm for a bite to eat. Look at him shake himself, he reminds me of the dogs I had. How I miss them! I miss owning animals. But why don't you like the country?"

"I jumped over a gate and went into a field to take a short cut, and then I hear this sound, and a bull was coming for me, so I ran. I wasn't even wearing anyfink red, so I don't know why he was cross."

"He just felt like it. He's a bull."

"That's why I don't like the country, you don't know what danger lurks around the next bend in the empty road!"

"What, you met a fellow with a shiv the other night in the wharf!"

"I could reason wiv a human bein', mate, or give him money, or dodge 'im, but the bull, there's no reasoning wiv him and if I was to wave a pound note in front of him he wouldn't care. When are you going back to the country? You keep saying you will, but you never do —why?"

"I have to find my sister."

"What? Your sister? What happened her?"

Pip outlined to Mike how he had lost Babs.

"I went back to the workhouse, but she wasn't there— they told me to go to a certain Laundry, and I met a man there who looked like a weasel. He told me my sister stole money, which I don't believe, and he didn't know where she was. And I don't know where else she could be."

"Maybe she went back to that place—the place where your brother is."

"No, I wrote to him, and he hasn't seen her either. He was furious I lost her and blamed me. But he hasn't come to look for her, because he doesn't care. No, really, he doesn't."

"Din't you tell me you 'ad a brother in America? What about 'im? Could your sister have gone over to 'im?"

"Not likely she'd have the fare over. Henry heard from Geoff. He's working as a labourer in New York. They want more and more high buildings there and he says that soon some will be higher than our St Paul's, which I don't believe. He gave me his address to write to him. I wrote but so far I haven't heard anything back."

"So what's next? About your sister, I mean?"

"I'm going to go around to all the workhouses."

"What about the police?"

"They took all her details but said there were hundreds of girls missing in London and were no help at all."

"Cheer up, me ole china. It's not bad. A lot of girls can look after themselves, you know?" He winked.

"What do you mean, Mike?" Pip looked at him with suspicion.

"Oh, nothing at all! No offence meant! But maybe your sister met an old Duke and is now in jewels and furs. Come on, I don't like to see you glum. You can't go about your whole life with a long face. Cheer up, mate."

Wherever Pip went, he kept his eyes open for Babs. Unknown to him, he passed her house in Holborn once. If he had known that she was there, safe, fed and sheltered with a kind mistress, he would have been a happy man indeed. His cares would have melted away and he would have turned his steps toward Essex without delay. But he did not, and he continued to search.

BABS IN SERVICE

Babs had been at the house now for six months when she decided that she would like to try something else. She tired easily, most likely because her illness had been severe. She had been very wise in spending her two sovereigns and used them to get herself a better wardrobe and boots. She purchased material and sewed at night. She scanned the master's newspapers when she was cleaning the parlour, before the butler retrieved them for himself, and took note of any hopeful situations by scribbling the postbox numbers in a little notebook she kept in her apron pocket.

One day her heart jumped when, as she was turning a page, she saw an advertisement for *Swann's Furniture in 10 - 12 Ferry Road, Whitechapel. All the best in fine furniture, mahogany, oak, rosewood, dressing tables, bed boards, dining tables and chairs*...now she knew where Caleb lived and worked! Had she really wandered that far that dreadful and wonderful Christmas Eve? She relived the events in her mind. She had never forgotten how she had felt when Caleb had swept her up in his arms and taken her to the hospital and how he had placed his hand on her head and told her that he would pray for her.

She scribbled the address down quickly in her notebook under the ones for *Mrs. G, companion needed—quiet house* —and *neat female tutor required for girl age 10, must know piano.*

"Babs, you're loitering, you should be finished a half-hour ago," scolded the housekeeper. "What are you doing with those newspapers? You're not throwing them out, are you? You know Mr. Hodson wants them."

"Oh yes, Mrs. Burke. For the racing." All the servants knew that the butler liked a flutter, but this had just slipped out, and she bit her lip. But her master had come in just behind Mrs Burke, and he said: "Hodson likes a flutter on the gee-gees! I never knew! Has he got any tips for Ascot?"

Before long Bets was offered another situation, one that promised her a comfortable home and light duties. She was to become a companion to a Mrs Grace, a genteel widow with no children, who lived on her own. For the interview at her middle-class home, she had to read to her and show her that she could sew and that she had some education. Mrs Grace liked music and Aunt Kitty's forcing her to practice was in her favour as Mrs Grace asked her to play for her. She was very pleased and offered her the position as she poured her a cup of tea in her neat, old-fashioned parlour.

"But your youth gives me a little hesitation," she said. "Pray what is your age?"

"I am seventeen." Babs did not like to lie and if she were to live with this lady, it was best to tell the truth. If she added a few years to her age she might forget and the truth could slip out and her employer be displeased.

"Seventeen—hmm. Young. A girl of your age should not want to be cooped up here with an older lady."

"You are not that old, Ma'am!" Babs smiled.

This seemed to please the lady for she laughed.

"What age do you think I am?" she asked her.

"Thirty, perhaps?" Babs was wise enough to take several years off what she really thought. She was about the same age as Aunt Kitty, and reminded her of her, which is why she felt at ease with her, perhaps.

"I am almost forty," she said. "I am strongly tempted in your favour, Miss Wren, for you remind me of my niece, who lives in Newcastle and teases me as you have just done. But how is it that you are so alone in the world, my dear?"

Babs had expected this enquiry.

"My father was a businessman who lost everything in a misadventure. My brother emigrated, and another lives in North Essex. I came to London with my third brother, Philip, but we have lost each other. I have been left without fortune and must earn my living."

"And your mother and father?" probed Mrs Grace.

"They are missing," she lowered her head. "Some think they abandoned us, but I know they did not."

Mrs Grace expressed her sympathy. There was a little pause. Babs worried that her unusual situation might influence Mrs. Grace against her. Her eye had fallen several times upon the portrait of a middle-aged gentleman on the wall, and she asked:

"Might I enquire if that is your late husband, Mrs. Grace?"

"It is he. My dear Maurice. He is gone only a year."

"I'm sorry for your loss. Were you very much in love?"

"Oh, of course! I could not marry without love."

"He looks like a very distinguished gentleman, and I see a kind twinkle in his eye."

"You see that? Now you know his nature. A kinder, happier man does not exist."

She asked her then if she would take the position, and then showed her her room. It was a small room, but well-appointed, and she thought it luxurious compared to what she had been sleeping in since that dreadful time when they had been driven from their home at Redgate. She moved in that day, but after settling her things about her, instead of being happy, she felt a desperation about her brother Pip. Where was he? In a chilly, stinking lodging? Did he even know she was safe?

Mrs Grace sat down to write a letter to her sister in Newcastle and received a reply a few days later to the effect that she was very foolish to take in a young woman as companion; she would be no end of trouble, and if she did not find her a husband, she would be stuck with her forever. *You should have chosen a paid companion your own age, but I suppose she admired Maurice, and that decided it.*

Oh Mildred, always worrying about something, she thought as she folded her letter, and yet—a young woman was a responsibility.

THE WORST NEWS

There were some days that Pip could not find work, and on those days, he resumed his search for Babs. He returned to Brownton Workhouse to no avail, and to the Laundry in case she had been back. The Weasel was out, and he was met by four buxom women who roared with hilarity when he introduced himself as Miss Wren's brother...oh no, they knew that trick, and they nudged each other and laughed until they seemed to be about to die of the joke and he stayed long enough to ascertain that she had not returned, a fact that was delivered without any cessation of laughter, and he went away.

Mike had told him to try lodging houses and so he began his trek—there were so many of them scattered about the East End, and many did not have signs on them. Of those he saw, he disliked the places so much he hoped that his sister had never had to bide in any of them. They housed coarse, slatternly women who smelled of gin and took too much interest in him rather than in his search for his sister, openly admiring him and soliciting attention.

Finally, he had a lead! One day in April, he came upon the first lodging house that Babs had stayed in. The landlady there, who he thought had a shifty look, said she had disappeared suddenly but that someone had seen her down by Fen Street, and there was a lodging house there for women, not as good as the one she ran here, mind you, it was a lot worse, and she should have stayed here, but she thought someone had done her ill, and she went off.

Fen Street was a dilapidated, run-down cul-de-sac ending in a narrow lane leading to a canal. There was a bad-smelling tannery there and across from that, several shabby houses with torn curtains and broken windows. He saw two women coming out from the door of one of them, their lips an unnatural red, and dressed in pert feathery hats and gaudy gowns. He shook his head. Was it even worth the knock on the door?

But they saw him and sidled up to him with a saucy air, lifting their hems a little too high to avoid the mud.

"Lookin' for company, guv'nor?"

"I'm not looking for company," he said shortly.

"Then why are you 'ere, in this street? Got business in the tannery, then, do you?"

It was impossible that his sister could be here.

"Speak again," urged one of the women. "I want to 'ear your accent."

"Really, I don't want to—"

But the sauciness had left this woman.

"It could be her brother," she breathed to her companion, poking her in the arm.

"Whose brother?" Pip asked quickly.

"She talks the same way. And I see a resemblance. She was looking for 'er brother. Are you Pip?"

Pip's heart leaped.

"Do you know my sister, Barbara—Babs? Is she here?"

But the women's faces fell. All levity had drained from their countenances. They hung their heads, and glanced at each other with lowered eyes, biting their red lips.

"Well, what's wrong? Where is she? How do you know her? Just tell me! Is she in there—is she—*as you are?*"

One of his worst fears was spoken, that Babs in her great necessity had taken up the oldest profession. He would never forgive himself!

"Oh no, she was not like us, wouldn't be like us."

"Put him out of his misery, Polly!"

"We're very sorry. Yes, we knew your sister, Babs. She was a very good girl, sweet and nice, and—"

"And she's dead," Jane said.

Pip's face whitened. He seemed about to collapse, but gathered himself together, and asked how it had happened.

"She had an accident. She was walking by the canal, and must have fell in."

"No!" he said. It could not be true!

"It is so, I'm afeard." The women nodded.

"Where did it happen? Will you show me?"

They walked with him to the bank where they had found her bonnet.

Pip was speechless, miserable.

"Why?" he asked. "How?"

"She was ill—on her way to the 'ospital—she must have been delirious, she must 'ave slipped in."

They talked to him for a while, telling him about Babs. He asked how she had earned money to keep herself.

"She was a singer, sang on street corners, took in good money sometimes, other times not so, but in the autumn with the fog and the damp, she became ill."

He thanked them. Anxious to be off, they left him at the canal bank, staring numbly at the spot where his sister had been lost.

There was no reason for him to stay in London now. He hated the place! It was spring in Hetherton. Everything bursting to life. The farmers needed help. He would set out tomorrow.

BABS'S DAYDREAMS

The paid companion ranked above a servant, for she was expected to greet and entertain guests and assist the employer in all her business and charities. Mrs. Grace had few outside interests and did not tax her companion too much. Babs would have preferred to have been busier. She fretted that she had no opportunity to look for Pip, for Mrs. Grace would be alarmed if she left the house for too long.

She led a comfortable if boring life, for Mrs. Grace's friends were all her own age, around forty, and thought they all admired and liked her and praised her music, and she could not meet anybody her age apart from the servants who she was not supposed to be friendly with. But she was eating well and looking well and grateful for the job and the comfortable home. Mrs. Grace was a lonely woman and they formed a bond of friendship, with the result that Babs told her a great deal more about herself. Mrs. Grace repaid her by confiding in her—she had a little girl who had died, and she would be Babs's age now if she had lived.

Mrs. Grace had a romantic heart and recounted her courtship by Mr. Grace with happy smiles born of cherished memories.

"I hope you find a good husband," she told Babs. "I will go out more this winter and take you with me." Even as she said it, she began to feel gloomy about having to go out on cold nights when she would much rather be by her fireside with a good book.

But Babs's heart was elsewhere. As autumn arrived her thoughts began to turn to Caleb. She wanted to see him again, and she wanted him to recognise her. She wondered how best to arrange this.

I will go to Swanns Furniture and tell an assistant that Mr. Dalton has a visitor—no—then our meeting would be very public—for I doubt he has an office or a workshop of his own—I will write to him and ask him if he knows whose life he saved last Christmas, and hint that I am from Hetherton, and let him guess—but no, that won't do at all, for I would not see his face, and what if he thought it was some sort of joke and threw the letter away?

She established two things in her heart, one was that she wished to let Caleb know who she was; the other—that she wished to see Caleb face-to-face, and the second wish was the strongest and the one that needed attention. She sat up in bed one night after tossing the question in her mind. The moon was shining in the window.

I will go to Swanns at the close of business on Christmas Eve—and meet him just as he is coming out. I will approach him and smile and say: Do you remember last Christmas Eve? There was a girl there on the ground, near death, and you rescued her. That girl was me. I am very grateful to you and want you to know that I am in health and fully recovered.

She wondered how long it would take for Caleb to recognise Babs Wren from Hetherton. Perhaps he would know her straightaway! Perhaps he would wonder why she was familiar! Perhaps he would not recognise her at all, and she would then say:

Do you remember one day on the downs at Hetherton, when a sparrowhawk chased a flock of starlings, and they swooped down among the sheep to hide at their feet? Who was with you at that moment?

She imagined the light of recognition come over his face and the spreading happiness at seeing her again—it would be joy—it must be!

From there Babs allowed her imagination to run freely. He would take her hands in his. After the initial revelation, he would say that he was going to get the train to Essex and—and—would she like to accompany him?

Oh yes, I would love t—but what would your parents think?

They would love to see you, and Alice too!

Then I shall come!

They would set off together for Liverpool Street Station, walking hand in hand—and it would snow of course, while they travelled—they would arrive to a beautiful scene of Christmas snow at Hetherton, and the country would never look more magnificent than when lit by the moon on the snowy hills and trees on Christmas Eve. He would hold her close as they walked through the snow to the Dalton cottage.

When I was a little child, Caleb, I used to imagine angels coming to your hillside to announce the birth of Jesus, and that you and your family would be the first to receive the news!

He would laugh, but not unkindly—Caleb was not unkind!

The familiar little cough Mrs Grace always gave after she blew out her candle in the next room brought Babs back to the real world.

*Oh dear, what of that dear lady? I will have disappeared, and she will be so worried! I wouldn't worry her for the world! Of course, all that is very unlikely to happen—we will renew our friendship, I will thank him and he will enquire my address here in London and he will go to Hetherton without me—and there won't be snow—but when he returns he will find me and...but what shall I wear to Swanns Furniture on Christmas Eve? Not anything like last year! My Sunday Best? Or maybe not...*as she pondered what to wear, a cloud drifted across the moon, the room darkened and she drifted into sweet slumber.

THE MEETING

Babs and Mrs Grace became good friends. They had compatible natures and felt very comfortable living in the same house. She told her shyly one November morning that she turned eighteen that day, and the day became one of celebration. As the Festive Season approached, she got the courage to ask for leave on Christmas Eve.

"Mrs Grace—I have an errand to do on Christmas Eve," she told her a week before Christmas. "It's something I need to do alone—I need to go alone."

"Oh dear! You should not go out alone, Babs. But I cannot stop you, for I'm your employer, not your guardian. You are eighteen years old now. Go if you must. But why can I not come along? If you wish to shop alone, I can go to another part of the shop—but do not get me anything extra dear, because the shawl you're embroidering for me is more than enough."

She began to feel a nervous anticipation as Christmas Eve approached and wished she could talk to somebody about what to wear. Mrs. Grace noticed her changed moods as she swung from excitement at seeing Caleb to the almost feverish wondering about her attire.

"What is it, Babs? Might I enquire?"

Babs decided to confide in her about her dreadful experience of last Christmas Eve and her rescuer. As she told her story the romantic sensibilities of Mrs. Grace were excited, and she fully supported Babs in her venture. In truth she was silently relived that Babs had a *beau*. She did not want to be responsible for launching her on society, and yet, while she remained in her house, she would feel obliged.

Together they planned her wardrobe—tasteful but not showy—bright but not gaudy. A simple ivory gown with crimson flounces, with a warm mantle over it in deep red. She wore her bonnet trimmed in ivory further back upon her head, showing more of her luxuriant hair and her face unshaded by the rim. The pimples were few now—would he know her?

"Oh, the time—I have no idea what time it was when I was there last year, all I know is that it was dark."

"All the shops close at six or earlier on Christmas Eve—but why do I not send Tom there and he will find out so we are sure."

The manservant Tom was duly dispatched and reported that Swanns Furniture would shut their doors at five o'clock to allow the staff to get home.

As they made their way there in the carriage, Babs took in the scenes outside—London's customary darkness and gloom banished for a few nights of light and jollity.

"This is Ferry Road, Ma'am!" said the cabman.

"Very well, we shall get out now. Don't worry, Babs, I'm not going with you—I shall linger and look in at the shop window while you meet him."

RETURN TO SWANNS FURNITURE

Babs could scarcely believe that one year ago she had dragged herself along this same street, only half-alive, and that now she was walking briskly along in happy anticipation of seeing the man she had been thinking about for the last year. Her heart beat rapidly—what if he was not here? What if he had Christmas Eve off to go home early? She banished the thoughts and anxieties, and then she was standing in the shopfront, at the very spot where she had sunk to the ground a twelvemonth before. She waited just a few minutes while customers came out, eyeing them narrowly, and pretending to look for something in her reticule.

Then—the door opened and a tall young man in a greatcoat and bowler hat emerged—she gave a little start—it was he! It was Caleb! He had not seen her—she gave a small step forward—and at that moment a fine carriage drew up and a young woman in a high and fancy hat put her head and her white-gloved hand out the window.

"Caleb!" she called to him. "We must make haste, for Aunt Lydia will be waiting! Dinner is at seven sharp!"

He stepped quickly past Babs and she, hardly believing what she was seeing, dropped her head to her chest in a rush of confusion and lest she be seen *now*.

But she had been noticed, not by him, but by the quick young lady in the carriage.

Her eyes went to her—and Caleb turned around to see what had gotten her attention.

Babs turned and slipped quickly away, her heart almost refusing to believe what she had seen.

Caleb got into the carriage and Miss Swann tucked her arm in his.

"Caleb, that was very odd, do you not think so?"

"Yes" …his eyes went to the window, and he saw that the girl had joined a woman friend and then he could see no more as the horses picked up speed.

"Who was she? Do you know her?"

"No, I don't."

But he suspected very strongly that it was the girl he had rescued last Christmas Eve. As did Miss Swann.

"Was it that girl who you took to the hospital last year? Did she return to thank you? But it could not have been her, for that girl—last year—from what Lady C told my mother, was from the very dregs of society, starving and near death—the rags barely covering her and no hat."

Caleb was filled with emotion at the memory. He clenched his hand beside him. His thoughts churned in his head—was it her? He had got a glimpse of dark hair under the streetlight. She had dark hair. She was about the same height. But more than that he could not determine.

"Well, we shall never know, I suppose." Miss Swann said cheerfully. "She could not go from being what she was last year to the well-dressed girl we just saw. Caleb? What is the matter? You seem dumbstruck."

"It was just so odd," he said.

"Yes, and now we shall forget it. Shall we announce our engagement tonight? Please say we can! What is there to wait for?"

"Tonight, then, Stella," he drew her close. But he did not want to kiss her, and he did not know why. But Stella did not notice. She was already planning the wedding for May next.

"To marry before Lent, that's too soon—I wouldn't be ready. So we shall have to wait until Easter, but then we might as well wait until May, which is my favourite month, and my cousins will be able to travel from

Scotland, I shall entreat them! Dearest, we shall be the happiest couple in the world!"

He held her, but his thoughts were elsewhere.

It shouldn't be like this, he thought. I should be as excited as she. I do love her, like her, but why do I feel so disturbed by a glimpse of the girl I'm sure was Miss White? Thank God she is alive, and healthy! And has a friend to look after her!

Stella prattled all the way to Kensington where they were to spend Christmas.

When the engagement was announced after dinner, Mr. Swann pumped his hand with a hearty shake. His countenance was beaming. But his wife's nephew, Harvey, was silently fuming. His hopes were sliding away. He felt an intense jealousy of Caleb Dalton, the shepherd's son from nowhere.

It was a Christmas like no other that Caleb had spent. A large house, fine meals, walks in frosty manicured gardens, he tried to look the part but did not feel it. There was a concert with a singer from Italy who was supposed to be famous, and he was utterly bored and thought her singing awful. There was a dance, and he was self-conscious. He never had a ballroom dance lesson in his life and Stella was teaching him how to waltz, but he would much rather have been dancing at Hetherton, prancing about to Old Mo's accordion, dressed in smock frock with bells attached to his leggings, instead of gliding about in a tight suit with Stella whispering *one-two-three one-two-three* to keep time to four screechy violins. He felt that the Vernons were laughing at him, and Harvey's glances at him while he conversed with his relatives convinced him that he was sneering at his efforts. *You can take the boy out of the country, but you can't take the country out of the boy.*

His mind, when it was not on Miss White, was on his home in Hetherton. It was the first Christmas without him, and he wondered how it was there. He missed them, and the neighbours, and how he used to roam around and see them all...their hearty welcomes at the doors: *'It's Chippy Dalton, come in!'* and catching up on all the news of everybody. They were simple people with big hearts, unlike the crowd he was with tonight.

When they returned to work, Mr. Swann called him aside and took him to the showroom, where he made his way through an array of furniture fit for the most elegant rooms, until he came to a rectangular rosewood table for six people. He tapped its polished top.

"I want to send your parents a gift," he said, beaming from ear to ear, "and this is what I've chosen, this table which is entirely your work. I will 'ave it packed up and sent as soon as we 'ave our pending orders fulfilled."

CHRISTMAS HEARTBREAK

When Babs had joined Mrs. Grace, that lady knew immediately that a great disappointment had overcome her companion, and that the man she hoped to meet was now in a carriage with a young woman by his side—that much she had seen and heard.

Babs's spirits were crushed. She had never anticipated this outcome. That he would not recognise her as Miss White had crossed her mind, but she had been sure that upon being told, and seeing her so healthy and well and smiling, he would be as happy as she. Then he would wonder how she knew his name! Mr. Dalton! But none of this had happened—instead, she felt like she had been drenched in cold water by a passing cart as had often happened to her when she was singing at a corner, only this time it was not her skirts and cracked boots that got soaked, but her spirit and her heart, and all her hopes.

Caleb. *She* had called him Caleb. There was an intimacy there. Unless she was treating him as an inferior—a servant. Babs clutched at straws but finally admitted that it could not be so: *'We must make haste, for Aunt Lydia will be waiting! Dinner is at seven sharp!'*

It was as it had looked to be—Caleb had been invited to spend Christmas with her family, whoever she was. Miss Swann? There had been talk of a Miss Swann before she had left Hetherton.

She could not keep the tears back. Mrs Grace did not attempt to quieten her. She was deflated also. Upon gaining their house Babs did not wish for company so she went to her chamber to cry herself out. What a Christmas Eve this had turned out to be—it started out happy and full of anticipation and ended in heartbreak.

Yet, she thought after a while, *if he is happy, I should be happy for him—I will be. Yes, I will be happy for him. I will myself to be happy for Caleb and his love. That will be my silent Christmas gift to him. He gave to me last year. Christmas is a time for giving, even when the giving requires sacrifice of the heart.* She dried her tears and returned downstairs sober and calm and told Mrs Grace of her intention.

"I'm pleased to see it, dear. Now this is Christmas, and we shall have a good, holy Christmas, for though you are very disappointed—and I feel so too—Our Lord and Saviour came on earth for us and we will be grateful and happy, or we will try to be. The first Christmas without Maurice I felt I could not be happy, and I was not, for he died only six weeks before, but I tried to be brave and go on, taking one day at a time, and I threw myself into helping the servants, and I'm not lecturing you, dear, I am trying to help. It is very hard."

Babs nodded and managed a brave smile. Her disappointment was not at all as bad as losing the person you loved day after day. She wouldn't miss Caleb, for she was never with him, but she would miss the constant thought and the hope of being with him someday.

"Thank you, Mrs. Grace." Babs even ate a good dinner and opened her gift from Mrs. Grace with joy. It was a fetching hat.

Christmas then passed with very little drama. On Boxing Day, she wore a kind smile for the servants and entered into their treat as fully as she could manage. None of them even guessed her sorrow. She cheerfully took her turn in the kitchen cooking and washing dishes while they had the day off. They had visitors on the day after that, and the day after that again they went visiting. Then it was New Year's Eve, and they rang in the New Year, and wished each other happiness. Her feelings were far from celebratory. She was putting a brave face on it in public, but in private her pillow saw many tears.

MRS. DEBORAH DELAMERE

Mrs. Grace had confided in her best friends that her young companion had been enamoured by a gentleman who was employed at Swanns Furniture, name of Dalton, but that she had suffered a disappointment before Christmas, but as to what had happened a year before that, she was silent, for that was too personal to share and she did not have Babs's permission to tell anybody about it.

One of these friends, a Mrs. Delamere, read the newspapers, and she hurried to Mrs. Grace early one morning to pay a call, the *Times* in her hands. There, Mrs. Grace read:

Mr. and Mrs. Thomas Swann of Ferry St, Whitechapel are pleased to announce the engagement of their daughter Stella to Mr. Caleb Dalton, also of Whitechapel, formerly of Hetherton, Essex. The wedding is expected to take place soon.

"I thought you would like to know," her friend said breathlessly. "The poor girl! Has he used her very ill? For as I see it, he is marrying into the family to inherit, for she will get all; I hear there is no son, only a nephew, who is undeserving."

"Gracious, Deborah, you have made enquiries, haven't you? But no, the gentleman has not used her ill. It was not as if they had an understanding. She knows him from before, and had romantic feelings in his direction, but they are not returned."

"Oh, you do not convince me, Phoebe, for I know it is the old story! He spoke love to her and kissed her by the garden gate, I'll warrant, for I know of these things, it happened to me with one Mr. Featherstone, then he saw Miss Parrott's money and was off. I shall go now, for you will want to tell her as soon as possible. Do you know that a little Portuguese wine is very good for disappointments such as this? Not too much, one glass only. I have some at home, shall I send it over? Indeed, I should have thought of bringing it, for he was a great cad. I am much happier with Mr. Delamere than I would have been with the cad, you may disclose that to her, that there is hope she will meet a better man, and richer than this Mr. Dalton will ever be. I never think of Mr. Featherstone now. Never."

"I'm sure there's no need to send over the wine, Debbie. I have wine here, should it be required."

Babs entered the room then, and Deborah, giving her a very sympathetic look, patted her on the shoulder, murmured something about heartless cads and left without calling the servant to let her out.

"What is wrong with her?" Babs asked, wonderingly. "Mrs. Grace, what is it? You look as if you have had a shock. Is everything all right?"

Mrs. Grace sat her down and handed her the newspaper.

"Here, my dear, read it. I am so very sorry."

The announcement brought a fresh shower of tears. Mrs. Grace ordered a pot of hot tea, which in her opinion offered a great deal more consolation than a glass of expensive Portuguese wine.

Later on, Mrs. Grace had an idea to distract her companion, and wondered how she had not thought of it before.

"Babs," she said, "why do we not place an advertisement in the newspapers to look for your brother Pip?"

This cheered her. Her dark eyes looked large and hopeful.

"Is that possible?"

"Yes, and I am a dunderhead not to have thought of it before now! We shall craft an enquiry tomorrow and I will send Tom to all the newspaper offices."

It was done, and they waited for responses, but in vain, for none at all came.

LETTER TO CALEB

Alice wrote to her brother regularly, but he was not so good at writing back. She usually kept her letters short, as she hated writing and was a poor speller, but when Pip returned to Hetherton with the dreadful news that Babs was dead, she grieved greatly and took pen to paper.

Dear Caleb, I have good news and bad news. Pip Wren came back from London—that's the good news. But I be sorry to tell you Babs is no more on this erth.

At this, Caleb startled in disbelief. Babs, the sweet lively girl he remembered, was no more? On his last visits to Hetherton when he had met her, he thought she had grown comely, and what was more, that she had a little shine for him, but he had not encouraged her, he was too young and had nothing to his name, and she was too young also. He reckoned she had been about fifteen to his twenty.

He read on, sitting on his bed, the sun slanting in the window.

He told me all about it. For he is very cutt up and blemes himself, and his brother Henry you kno is no good at all. What happened was this—Pip and Babs come to london and cud not find work and Babs had to go to a work-hous. He was ashemed to tell me that, but I udnerstand how it can be if you are far away from home and no work or food and the rain poring down. He did the right thing, though babs fout him on it. He visit her, and then one Sunday she was gone, to work in a laundre but left that because Pip said they are all mad there, mad as hatters with a wesel in charge. He looked and looked for her and nothing turned up and then he met a few girls who nowed her and they said that she was dead of a fever. That's all he tol me. I cud not get any more out of him becose he was too cutt up and blemes himself for all of this. If they had staid with Mr. Henry it wud have been all right for them but they hated it there and they were treated very badly.

After he read this letter, Caleb went for a long walk. His mind was full of memories of Babs and indignation that Pip had not confided in him when they had met down by the docklands.

It's obvious she was missing then—I could've helped him look for her—why did he not confide in me? We were all friends together when we were young!

He concluded that Pip was embarrassed about abandoning his sister to a workhouse, and ashamed of what he perceived to be his stupidity or neglect. He would not admit it to Caleb, nor to anybody, he supposed, but to his sister Alice. Pip and Alice had always been good friends. Alice had a way of drawing people out. Perhaps Pip even now did not wish him or anybody else to know, but Alice could not keep this to herself. The workhouse was a great shame indeed.

As he walked along a dilapidated street, he heard somebody play a mouth organ, albeit very badly. He remembered with a rueful smile the one he had given to Babs, the one which had secured his apprenticeship. He went in search of the player, to find a girl aged about twelve playing it for passersby, and her brother, about six years old, holding out a hat for pennies.

He flipped a few pennies into the hat before he got a glimpse of the mouth organ. It was the one he had made—the inlay was unmistakable.

"May I see that?" he asked her. She showed it to him.

"Where did you get it?" he asked the girl, and his urgent manner frightened her.

"Hey Mister, I din't nick it! It's mine!"

"I'm not saying you nicked it. But where did you get it?"

"I got it from a cabbie."

"A cabbie! Did you take a ride then, in a cab?"

"Oh no, Mister. Me in a cab indeed! I did 'im a service, Mister, his cab got all covered in mud inside from dirty boots, and I washed it and I found that under the seat, and he said to keep it."

"Do you know where the cabbie is now?"

"Oh no sir, we never seed him again arter that."

Caleb dug his hands into his pockets and brought out five shilling coins.

"I'll give you this, for that mouth organ," he said. "You can buy a much better one. But I'd like that one, because I know who it belongs to. Now go and get yourselves a nice eel pie an' mash to eat. Don't lose the money."

The children were delighted with the bargain and the mouth organ was handed over to Caleb. He turned it over in his hand, looking at it and finally he put it in his pocket.

He would take it to Pip on his summer visit home to Hetherton. It would be a little consolation for him, maybe.

PIP AND ALICE

Had Pip still been in London, somebody might have shown the Missing Persons advertisement to him, but he had been largely forgotten by the big city as soon as he had left. He had been in Hetherton for nine months now, had worked hard all spring, summer and autumn as a labourer on the farms, eating with the servants and living in barns. As Christmas had approached, he had not known what to do. He had nowhere to go and felt the loss of his family very keenly.

About that time Mr and Mrs Dalton got the unwelcome news that Caleb was staying in London for the Festive Season. They and Alice were very disappointed.

"Ma, let's ask Pip Wren for Christmas. He has nobody. Let's do 'im this kindness," Alice said.

Pip had spent Christmas in the Dalton cottage, and while nothing could compare with the company of their own

Caleb, with his tales of London and his gifts and bright presence, he was a great addition. He was helpful, considerate and polite, even if sadness reigned in him. As work was lean on the farms just then, he offered to help out the Daltons for a time, so he stayed on.

"I never knowed he was so humble, poor chap." Dolly said. "He was always a nice lad, even when he was rich, but I see now that he's a good lad too. What do you think, Alice?"

"I think he should live with us, Mother. Father is getting on."

"Live with us! Oh, now Alice! I know what you mean, Miss!"

"We want to get married, Ma. Papa needs help, you need help. I want a husband, Pip wants a wife and a home."

"I don't know if he's for you, Alice, though I like the lad. Poor Pip is as poor as a dormouse."

"But Ma, he's asking Pa for my 'and, he was to do it this morning in the sheepfold. Please, Mama, I love him and he loves me. I never saw him in that way before, but he is the dearest, sweetest man, just the man to make me 'appy and I will make him 'appy, for we understand each other perfectly. We want to marry soon."

"And all this happened at Christmas under our noses! Ah, 'ere is your father now, so we will hear all. He has a letter or something in his hand. What could it be? What is it, Alf?"

Alf came in with a gust of cold air, and he shut the door quickly.

"I was handed this letter a while ago. It's from our son Caleb."

"Give it here, Pa, I'll read it out," cried Alice.

Dear Mother, Father and Alice, I hope you are well. I am writing to tell you of my eng- Here, Alice paused. It was a long word and if it was what she thought it was, she wanted to get it right.

"What is it?" asked her mother. "Is it *engagement* you're trying to say?"

"Yes, Ma." She resumed: *My engagement to Miss Swann. We became engaged on Christmas Eve. Her parents are very happy and I hope you will be too. She wishes to come and meet you all, and when the weather is better, we will undertake a journey to Hetherton. I hope to receive your blessing and congratulations, yours etc your loving son and brother, Caleb.*

There was a stunned silence in the cottage.

"Are you sure that's what it says? No joking now, Alice!"

"Would I joke about something like that, Father? Yes, it's all true!"

"Does he say her Christian name? Or did I miss hearing it?" asked her mother.

Alice cast her eyes back over the letter.

"No, he doesn't say. Isn't that a bit odd now. He must have forgot."

"Two weddings this year, then." Dolly said. "Alf, do you know what Alice here just told me?"

"I can make a guess. Pip asked me for her hand only an hour ago. I said yes, but against my better judgement, for he has nothing for her. Well, daughter, did I say the right thing?"

"Oh, you did, Father!" Alice rushed to embrace him. "We're all going to be so happy! If he can live here, he can work as under-shepherd with you. He already asked Mr. Withers."

"Yes, he told me that. You'll never be rich, daughter. A shepherd's pay."

"Oh, but Pip told me that he will tutor children, he went to school until he was sixteen."

"Perhaps that older brother of his will step up and 'elp his own," Alf said.

"When is Caleb getting married, and will we go to London for the wedding?" Dolly Dalton mused. "For I don't think we can all afford to go, not all of us, and then there are the clothes, better just you go, Alice."

"I can borrow Cousin Lily's blue plaid calico. Pip will get a suit from somebody. It will be a fancy affair, Mama, I think." Alice said.

"I don't like the sound of it then," Dolly said decidedly.

"Mama, he's not throwing himself away though, like you feared, is he? Isn't this what you wanted for Caleb?"

"For him to have enough, and help us out a bit if we need...if she loves him and is good to him and attends to his wishes, and he to hers. But they are so different. He will have to fit in with her life."

"Then Pip and I are a good match, for we are both the same—poor," Alice said. ruefully. "Oh, I see him coming down the hill! Let's 'ave some tea!"

There was jubilation when Pip entered. He let in a gust of chilly air, and he fastened the door after him. He looked around him to see the reaction to the news that he and Alice were to marry. Mrs. Dalton got up and embraced him.

"We're all going to be 'appy together, I know it," Alice said. "Come and sit down, Pip, we're going to have tea."

Caleb kept them supplied in tea; they no longer had to re-use the leaves, and they loved the luxury.

Pip met her eyes. They spoke love. They clasped hands under the table at teatime and moved themselves closer to each other.

"We should look the other way, Alf," Mrs. Dalton chuckled. "Don't leave it too long for the wedding, you two! I wonder when Caleb is going to bring Miss Swann here. I hope he gives us notice, for I'll borrow some dishes and suchlike from Redgate House and we'll all 'ave to spruce ourselves up."

ANOTHER RETURN

P ip and Alice went for a stroll every evening, wrapped around each other, along a frosty laneway that led to the stream, the dog trotting along too. Pip carried a hurricane lamp. They heard the train come into the station. A familiar sound, it was the last train from London for the day, and after the passengers got off and went to their homes the village settled down for the night, with hardly a stir until daylight, the only sound being the dogs who barked every so often at the nocturnal creatures.

One frosty evening Alice noticed that Pip was quiet, and remarked it.

"Of what you be thinking?" she asked him, as the train was heard just a mile away.

"Babs, Geoff, Ma and Pa." He said quietly. "And Henry—he blames me for Babs. I blame myself too. Geoff seems to have vanished also. America is a big place, maybe my letter to him didn't reach him. The one telling him that Babs is no more."

"He knows Babs was missing, though, didn't he?"

"Yes, Henry had a letter from him after that. He was very cut up about it."

The moonlight shimmered on the stream, and they were silent for a time. It was a comfortable silence.

"We'll have children, won't we?" Pip said, squeezing her fingers.

"I'll give you five sons and five daughters!"

"I'll have to build us a mansion!"

As they walked back to the cottage, they heard someone come along the road, probably having come from the railway station. The countryside had an enveloping darkness, and they could only hear his steps, the long strides of a man. They saw no light. There was no house beyond the Dalton cottage, so Pip called out to him.

"Heyday. Whither going? Are you lost?"

The voice from the darkness startled him.

"Pip! Is that you?" the voice sounded elated.

"Yes, it is, but who—"

"It's Geoffrey! I was coming to the cottage to enquire of the Daltons as to where you might be found! And you're the first person I see since the station! My brother Pip! Is there any news of Babs? Is she found? I couldn't bide over there, not knowing. Who is that with you?"

The brothers were overjoyed to see each other again. Pip held the light up to his brother and proclaimed him as ugly as ever, which Geoff roared at and landed a mock punch on Pip's shoulder.

"Come in, Geoff," Alice took the lamp and led the way to the cottage.

"But what of Babs? Any news?" Geoff asked again after being greeted warmly by the old couple and told he could bide the night there. He had brought a loaf of bread, a pot of jam and a packet of cold boiled ham. They thought he had done well in America.

Pip told him the bad news. There followed sorrow and grief for a time, until the old couple asked questions about New York, which he was glad to answer, and he recounted anecdotes from his voyage.

"I'm home for good. I'm not going to America again. I'll get farm work in the spring. I have a few pounds to tide me over till then. Oh, it is good to be home in England! If only—" he did not have to finish the sentence. If only the family was together again.

Geoff slept in the cottage for a few days and made himself useful, and then left. He promised to keep in touch—nobody would separate him from Pip again, and all was quiet in Hetherton again, until another exciting arrival occurred.

THE ROSEWOOD TABLE

One showery afternoon after the train had come and gone, a breathless lad presented himself at the cottage, eyes wide in his head, with news.

"Mrs. Dalton! The station master says there's something for you at the station, it came on the London train, and you need a cart to bring it up, it's that big!"

What a mystery! Before any time at all had passed, the entire village was expecting to see this wonder. At the first opportunity Alf and Pip tackled the donkey to the cart and set out, while the women looked out the door every minute after a quarter-hour had passed, so impatient were they. Then there was a hue and cry; they beheld Neddy labouring up the lane, pulling something high and upright in the cart; the men beaming as they helped push it up the slope and a flock of noisy boys and girls eagerly running alongside and behind. The women ran out to meet the astounding procession.

"What is it? Does it say? Are you sure it's ours?"

"It's a table! From Swanns Furniture! *With the compliments of Mr. Swann, Master Cabinet Maker, in anticipation of the happy event to come. Your son Caleb designed and made this rosewood dining table. It is a fine example of his craftsmanship. Yours, etc, Thomas Swann."* Pip read out the accompanying note.

"Caleb made this here table! I can't wait to see it!" exclaimed the proud Mama as the wrappings were torn off to reveal an elegant polished reddish-brown surface.

"It's too big. It won't fit in the door." Alice was very disappointed. "We'd have to saw off the legs, and we can't do that to it."

"After we've had a look at it, we'll have to make room for it somewhere, it'll 'ave to be the shed. Stack it on its side against the wall, move the turf and sticks over from it. When we do the thatching, we can let it down through the roof." Dolly ran her fingers over the polished wood. "Look at the shine on it, did you ever see the like?"

"And the legs, with fancy twirls!" Alice marvelled.

"It be a very fine piece of stick!" Alf exclaimed. "And our son made 'n! But would he not know 'n wouldn't fit? For e'en if we let 'n down through the roof, 'n take up all the space inside! There be no space for dresser nor chairs even, nor anything else and we'd be walking around 'n to go from one end of the room to th' other; no, the table will 'ave to stay outside, more's the pity."

MISS SWANN VISITS

It was a March day when Caleb brought his bride-to-be to meet his parents. Unfortunately, he had not given them any notice. It so happened that the sun shone one day after two weeks of steady rain, and his fiancée thought that a trip to the country would be beautiful. She asked her father to give Caleb the afternoon off, and he assented. It ran into Caleb's head that his mother wanted notice, but Stella was so keen on going that he dismissed the thought and caught her excitement.

"I can't wait to meet your family," she told him. "Especially your sister Alice. I've always longed for a sister! And she is the same age as me!"

They brought her mother's maid as chaperone and alighted the train at Hetherton after a very pleasant journey, and when they were walking through the village a child ran up to Mrs. Dalton to tell her that Caleb was coming with a lady. She was kneeling in the vegetable patch planting seed potatoes. She groaned inwardly and sent the child to look for Alice who was with the lambs.

Dolly came hastily into the cottage and hurriedly rinsed her hands. She barely had time to change her apron for a clean one and tuck her hair under her cap before she looked out and saw them approach.

Since she had stepped out of the train, Miss Swann had been full of compliments about all she saw and felt. The air was clean and fresh; the spring flowers pretty; the hills charming! And all so peaceful! She looked about her to see the houses and guess which one was the Dalton's. She chose a good two-storey belonging to the butcher; "No," said Caleb, laughing, "that's not it." Then she picked the rectory. Lastly, she espied Redgate House on the top of the hill.

"Is it that handsome one?"

"Oh no, it's not at all as large as that," Caleb answered, losing a little of his exuberant mood. "I told you, it's a cottage."

"I thought you were teasing! But cottages are sweet and cosy. I can't wait to see which cottage it is!"

She hoped it was the tall one with attic rooms and creeping vines outside the window, but no. That belonged to the schoolteacher. Caleb seemed a little tense, so she stopped guessing.

They were now turning up a narrow lane toward a hill dotted with sheep, and out of a jungle of overgrown trees and bushes came a poor, small cabin with a roof of coarse thatch which a winter of rain had damaged and caused to sag in several places.

Surely it's not that, she thought, with dismay, and the chaperone had the same thought. They espied a woman dressed like a servant looking out the door, and hastily go back inside. All were silent as they turned in the gate and walked up the cracked path to the door she had seen the woman at. It was left a little open.

Caleb rapped on it and shouted—"Hallo Ma? It's me, Caleb! I have brought my fiancée!" He opened the door. He bent his head to go in, for he was taller than the door, which was almost the height of the house itself. The cage frame of Stella's crinoline skirt had to bend to allow her in the door—that humble door had never seen a skirt that wide, and a red hen got underneath her skirt, and squawked until she escaped.

Out of the light, and into the dark of the cottage, she was unpleasantly surprised.

A GIANT YELLOW LAMPSHADE

Small and miserable were the words that entered her mind as she took in her surroundings. Low class, so low! A deal table in the middle of the brick floor, a few plain chairs, a spinning wheel by the window, a basket of fleece, a dresser with assorted mugs and plates and a jug and basin, short, stubby candles, a bundle of sticks by the fire, cheap blue curtains on the small windows, an old chest covered by a faded blanket. Only one floor, with two rooms leading off this one on either side of the fire to what she assumed were very small bedchambers. And a smell of dog and something else—the cottage had a damp mustiness. The woman she had seen was standing before her—the word that jumped into her mind was 'peasant'. Her fiancé's mother was a *peasant,* and she was marrying into a peasant family.

"This is my mother. Mother, this is Miss Swann—Stella."

"I am that happy to meet you," Dolly said with the formality reserved for her betters. Her hands were folded in front of her old, well-washed apron of coarse cotton, for there was a frayed area on the pocket. She curtsied. "Please be seated by the fire. It's not a very good fire. I was out planting potatoes, for it will rain maybe."

Miss Swann told her chaperone to leave them—it was crowded enough, and Jennings was quite happy to walk out and down the road toward the village where there was something of interest to see. The conditions from which the favoured apprentice had come from appalled her.

Miss Swann was seated in the best wicker chair, and her pale yellow gown spread out in such a wide area that it bumped against the table. She tried to bring her skirts back as far as possible from the open fire, but with her cage underneath, it was impossible. Caleb told her to get up and he pulled the chair—it was his father's chair—as far back from the hearth as was possible.

"You should have told me you were coming," his mother quietly reproached her son.

Caleb was sorry now that he had given in to Stella's impulse. He had lived in London for so long that he had forgotten that his family home was small and poor and that there was never any ready food for guests. He always thought of it as a warm, welcoming place but they prepared too for his twice-yearly visits. He berated himself silently.

"But where is the table—Mrs. Dalton, the table that Caleb made? Did not my father send it?"

"Oh, yes and we did write a letter to thank him, it was so kind of him, but a beautiful table it is—it is all wrapped up safely in the shed. It's too big for the room."

"Oh." Stella said.

Caleb berated himself again. It pained him to think that it had not occurred to him that one of the smallest dining tables in the showroom was too large for his parents' cottage.

"When we get a bigger house, then we'll use it." Dolly said lightly. "For it is a very beautiful table, indeed it is, and a credit to you, son."

Mrs Dalton made small talk with her new guest. Did she find it a long journey from London? How were her parents? She admired her gown and said she had never seen anything so wide.

"Crinolines are all the rage," said Stella. "Do not think this one is wide, Mrs. Dalton, for I have seen many wider. There is a designer named Worth, Charles Worth, and he made them very popular. The French court are wild about them, they set the fashion and all follow suit. There is a new colour named mauvine, and I meant to have a gown made in it—I will be married in mauvine!"

"And what colour is that?"

"A sort of light purple, it's all the rage."

"I see, a sort of light purple..." Mrs. Dalton seemed lost for words. She had not had a new gown for decades, and new, expensive dyes were not in her budget.

"How is the lambing?" Caleb got up suddenly, changing the subject.

"We lost a ewe last night. She had twins, poor little mites. Alice is at the hut, keeping them warm."

"I'd love to see the lambs!" Miss Swann exclaimed.

"She'll be down any minute," Dolly wondered what on earth was keeping her daughter. She did not know what to say to this fashion plate from the big City. To think that she was to be her son's wife was something she could not take in at present.

Just then Stella winced and let out a little scream, and brushed something off her shoulder that out of the corner of her eye she had seen fall past her head.

"Don't worry, I have him." Caleb was by her side, and held an insect between his finger and thumb, which he disposed of under his foot upon the floor.

At that moment the door flew open, and a breathless Stella entered. She had had the foresight to go directly to the village and beg the baker for six little cakes on credit, and had run back. A snooty-looking stranger in bonnet and cloak had also been there, and she thought she might be part of the visiting party and was ashamed of her own appearance.

Another unpleasant surprise was in store for Stella. Her sister-in-law-to-be cut a very disappointing figure. Her full cheeks were red, her cap was askew, her apron stained with a variety of blotches. She smelled of the animals. She put down the box, wiped her hands on her apron and took the cakes out.

A cup of tea was brewed, and then they went to see the lambs and to meet a surprised Alf, whose first glimpse of his future daughter-in-law was to see his son helping what he said later was a giant yellow lampshade over a stile.

Stella had seen enough of his family before she met Mr. Dalton, the tall, gaunt shepherd with wild white hair, dressed in his customary smock-frock and leggings and quaint in his speech. The shock of the last two hours made her silent on the journey home, though she pleaded fatigue from all the walking. Caleb was quiet also, and the maid looked with contempt at him out of the corner of her eye. Was Miss Swann out of her mind?

Stella told her mother tearfully that night that she could not believe that this handsome man could come from the 'squalor' she had seen, to think that those people were his parents! That girl his sister!

"You should not have gone unannounced," her mother

said. "That was very bad of Caleb! But typical of a man, I suppose."

"I don't think we can marry this year, Mama. I'm simply unsure now."

"Take your time, dear. You are still young, and perhaps it's a good thing this happened."

"What shall I say to Papa? He wants it so much!"

"Say nothing for the present. If he enquires about the delay, I will tell him you still feel too young for the responsibilities of marriage."

Mrs. Swann had asked Jennings what she had thought, and she had left her in no doubt as to the unsuitability of this marriage.

CHIPPY ON HER MIND

Pip and Alice were married just after Easter in the village church in a very simple but sweet ceremony. Caleb attended, but his fiancée did not, pleading illness. Mrs. Dalton was happy in one way about that and unhappy in another, for she was a great catch and her son would never be in want. She did chastise him about bringing his fiancée to visit unexpectedly when they all looked their worst in the middle of a working day and lambing season at that. He had long since repented of it! Even Mrs. Swann had chided him that "it hadn't been at all fair on his dear mother, no mother-in-law-to-be would like that." His gentlemanly nature would not allow him to tell her that it had all been Stella's idea.

Caleb had his own doubts about the engagement. He sometimes thought he loved Stella, and sometimes not, but he doubted more and more if they had enough in common to make their life together happy. It was a complicating factor that he worked for her father and now had shares in Swann Furniture. But even if that was not a consideration, it was not done for a decent man to break the engagement. That was hers to do, for to stigmatise her with rejection would affect her chances with other suitors. He was therefore obliged to continue until she ended this, and she often gave him strong hints, and he felt it would be sooner rather than later.

Every time he walked near St. Bartholomew's Hospital he thought of the girl he had saved, and wondered how she was and if their paths would cross again. Miss White! How many Miss Whites in London!

Less than three miles away, the girl he knew only as Miss Anne White had plunged herself into charity work with her employer. It was a great way to heal a broken heart, and she was healing. Her smiles returned, and she resolved to forget Chippy Dalton completely, but her resolve was not as strong as she would have wished.

As the seasons changed and autumn rolled in, her mind turned to the last two Christmasses she had spent and what had happened.

I still have not thanked him. He would like to know that I am well. For to pick someone up off the street and carry them to a hospital—that would not be easily forgotten—if I had saved someone's life, I would always wonder how they got on.

Mrs. Grace's friend Mrs. Debbie Delamere had been keeping an eye out for the nuptials in the *Times,* and when day after day she saw no mention of the names Swann and Dalton, she began to suspect that no marriage had taken place and that it had all come to nothing. Serve the cad right! Miss Swann saw through him! These sentiments were delivered in rapidity to Mrs. Grace when her young companion was not present, and though she did not encourage them, it occurred to Phoebe Grace that perhaps all was not well between the engaged couple, for few couples waited this long, and if one put an engagement in the newspaper, the nuptials always followed in due time.

Babs became a little fidgety coming up to Christmas, and finally one morning at breakfast, she blurted out: "I still feel, Phoebe, that I ought to thank my rescuer." She waited for all the reasons as to why she should not do so, getting her hopes up, etc., but they did not come. Instead Mrs. Grace said:

"You could write, I suppose."

"Oh, that would not do at all, I feel so detached when I write a letter, I can't do that."

"So...you wish to thank him in person."

"Yes—just a quick thank you and let him know that I am fully recovered and well—and then I will be off."

"I can see that you won't be at ease until you do it, so will it be Christmas Eve again, then?"

"I think it would be a good time, for he might just remember Christmas Eve two years ago, and it might be on his mind, and then for me to pop forward and say 'thank you, you see, I am very well now!' It would be very good. And that's all, Phoebe, for I know he is married, and after I have done this, there won't be any more contact, and I shall cease forever to think of Chippy Dalton."

"Chippy Dalton! We shall go, then, if you wish it."

"I can even bear seeing his wife draw up in the carriage, to collect him to bring him to dinner. I will smile at her."

"Very good," Mrs. Grace had no intention of letting her know that it was possible that Caleb Dalton was still single. Her secret hope was that he would impart it, that is, if he was interested in her.

So, the red mantle was chosen again, and the red bonnet with ivory trim that framed her face, and again Mrs. Grace accompanied her and waited, looking in the windows at the tables and chairs while she went forward to the door just before five o'clock.

CALEB IS THANKED

This time, she was calmer. She had no expectations. He was married, and she was fulfilling her obligation to thank him for the service he rendered her two years ago. And then, while she was persuading herself that she would walk away with the contented feelings she had now, the door opened, and Caleb Dalton appeared. She stilled her heart and moved forward—no carriage this time to distract him! Good, though she had fully intended to nod and smile at Mrs. Caleb Dalton.

He paused, his eyes cast about and fell upon her.

There was a silence for a split second, before they began to talk together.

"Miss White, is it not?" He was smiling, a gentle smile, a very pleased smile. He bowed a little. Mrs. Grace saw it, she was watching them. Her hopes rose.

"Mr. Dalton. I owe you my life."

And then sudden tears sprung to Babs's eyes. Oh dear, this was not planned! She remembered well the tears of the carriage! She swallowed, but he had seen the tears, and her effort.

"You remind me of somebody—" he said.

She was not about to tell him who she really was, because then there would be animated conversation and her heart would fly all over again to his, and they would speak of Alice and the sheep and everything and she might never get her heart back, and he was a married man!

"I came last year to thank you, Mr. Dalton, but I did not wish to intrude, when the carriage came."

"I guessed it was you, Miss White. I'm very happy to see you well."

"So, I just wished to thank you—I won't delay you—I'm sure you're rushing home this Christmas Eve, to your family—"

"Yes, I am—how did you know?"

"It is where everybody is bound today, is it not? Goodbye then, and Merry Christmas to you—and to Mrs. Dalton."

"Well, yes, thank you—and to you—"

She fled rather too quickly, overcome with emotion,

unable now to contain the tears, and did not hear his last words—

"My mother, yes, how do you know—?"

She had meant of course his wife, but Caleb was too slow to see that. He continued his journey to Liverpool Street Station, for he was not spending this Christmas with the Swanns. It was clear to everybody except Mr. Swann that it was only a matter of time before the engagement was called off by Stella, and he accepted the excuse that Caleb wished to spend Christmas at home with his family.

"You spoke to him!" Mrs. Grace was elated. "Oh now, Babs, no tears! You said—"

But Babs was weeping. "I remembered that I was so near death—and I remembered how he took me up in his arms and remarked I was like a feather, or something, and that's all, he is gone now to spend Christmas with his wife, he is a happy married man, and she loves him. Now I'm quite ready to forget him completely. It is done, it is over, he knows I am well and happy, and he is thanked." She blew her nose into her handkerchief and regained her composure. They then went home to celebrate Christmas as they had done the year before.

Mrs. Grace was puzzled. She had seen him in the light of the streetlamp. His eyes had lit up, his smile had been that of a lover. She had seen wonder, enchantment even, in his countenance. He had sought to detain her, looked after her, his hand reaching out as if to draw her back! But she had rushed away...

She doubted very much that he was married, and she did not know what to do about it.

STELLA NAMES THE DAY

It was four months later, and Caleb and Stella were still officially engaged. It was as if she were afraid to let go in case she was making a mistake. She admitted to herself that it was his good looks that held her in thrall more than anything else, that and the very real fear of disappointing her father and all his plans for the business.

There were few men in London, in her opinion, who could match Caleb in looks. She resolved therefore to marry him and be done with it. They did not have to visit Hetherton. They could live a separate life in London, or if he insisted, Chelmsford, though she thought it must be a very provincial town and not at all lively, though she had never seen beyond the railway platform.

Caleb had thought about Miss White all through the Christmas before and well into the New Year and regretted that he had not made more of an effort to detain her in conversation, but she had been anxious to rush away. He felt he knew her from somewhere but could not tell. He went over all of his female acquaintances in London, all of his employer's daughters and their friends, Stella's friends and their sisters, their customers' daughters—but had no satisfaction.

Stella came to see him in the workshop, a barn-like hall with numerous pieces of machinery and benches for several woodworkers. It was chock-a-block with planks and furniture in various stages of manufacture. Just-begun, half-finished, or almost-finished pieces were everywhere. There was a smell of timber and varnish and turpentine.

Stella was dressed prettily in pink and white, and he acknowledged that she often looked attractive to him. She had a parasol and twirled it about.

"Caleb, I think we should name the day soon."

Caleb was applying a veneer to a walnut cabinet. He put down the veneer and came toward her but could not take her hands because of the oil on his.

"When is soon?"

"Next month. When the cherry blossoms are out."

"May then," he said.

"May 16th," she said, and after another few words passed between them, she left.

So, it is done, he thought, returning to his work. *I have to marry sometime, and I like her, and she likes me, and everything will be all right.*

Miss White's beautiful face framed by her dark hair drifted into his mind. He drove it away. He would most likely never see Miss White again.

MR. SWANN'S ILLNESS

Mr. Swann came to his workbench the following day, pumped his hand again, and said he would be the happiest of men with his daughter. He seemed breathless.

"Are you well, sir?" he asked him curiously, for he had a strange grey colour.

"I am quite well, thank you, happy, very happy indeed, to know that by the summer, you will be my son-in-law."

But as he was leaving the workshop, he halted by a workbench, put his hand out to steady himself, and slid to the sawdust floor.

The men rushed forward. A doctor was called for, and a board obtained to place him upon to carry him to his own bed.

"There must be absolute quiet, and no excitement," instructed the doctor. "His lungs are very congested, and his heart could be affected."

Mrs. Swann and Stella were dreadfully upset and nursed him with devotion. A wedding next month was out of the question now.

Only Harvey remained indifferent. He made a cutting remark to Caleb.

"The old man is out of your way now, isn't he? But I'll fight you for the business, for it's mine by rights."

"Be quiet, the women will hear you. Have you no consideration for them?"

Mr. Swann was unable to leave his bed and relied heavily upon his wife and daughter for everything. Caleb visited him for instructions about the business, and Harvey became more jealous with every passing day, for he was never called to his bedside. Harvey had no occupation. He had no interest in the business beyond the monetary gain it would bring him. He slept late, his valet took two hours to get him properly dressed, for he was a great fop. He lunched, and then about three o'clock he went to his club or to the homes of some of his friends where as long as he had money to throw about, he was made welcome. The evenings were spent with fine dinners, clarets, women and cards, and he returned home around three in the morning. His valet waited up for him and got him ready for bed. He was a bitter, unhappy man and thought that his uncle had used him ill. He was fond of his aunt, but she was also under the old man's thumb.

For the rest of the year Harvey waited for his uncle to die. He wanted to deal with Dalton but was afraid while the old man was still breathing. The summer brought an improvement, and Mr. Swann was able to sit out in the back garden in the afternoons, but when autumn set in, the fog and damp did its work in his lungs and in November, he fell gravely ill. It was to be his last illness.

Caleb visited him upon his request, and his last words to him were: *Be good to my Stella.*

He promised that he would. He thanked his mentor for taking a chance with him when he was only fourteen years old, but Mr. Swann did not want to be complimented.

"I knew you would do very well," he said to him. "Stella will inherit my shares in the business. You will be in charge of the workshop and the design department. For the business end, I recommend you employ a good man with experience, and not Harvey—he will want it—but do it at your peril. He will ruin you all."

He asked to see Harvey.

His wife's nephew was all agitation in the sickroom. What would the old man say to him? "For my wife's sake, I have provided for you. You can easily live off the interest of five thousand pounds."

Harvey disagreed, but did not say so. The old man had no idea how expensive it was nowadays to live as a gentleman should, but then he had never been a gentleman.

"You are not to have any part of the business. A condition of your getting the five thousand is that you sell your shares to your aunt."

Harvey fumed. But he said: "Yes, sir."

The conversation was over; no words of endearment were uttered on either side, and he left the room and descended the stairs. Caleb was in the hall, and he shot him a look of hatred.

It did not go well for him with Mr. Swann, Caleb thought. *What will he do when I refuse him the position he wants?*

Mr Swann struggled on until November's end, and breathed his last one frosty night with his wife and daughter by his side.

MOURNING

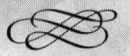

The house was turned into one of mourning. Dressmakers came with yards of black crape to make mourning clothes. The funeral was very well attended, for Mr. Swann was a popular man in his business and the prestigious furniture makers came to pay their respects.

Harvey approached Caleb as they were preparing to leave the graveside.

"I won't have shares in the business, Dalton, for I have to sell mine to my aunt, but I insist upon being in the office. I will be Director."

"Mr. Swann isn't even cold in his grave, Vernon, and you bring up this subject?"

"I lose no time, so that when it comes to choosing your Director, you will think of me. Nobody else."

"I refuse to discuss it here," Caleb joined Stella and her mother who had walked a little way ahead. There was a young gentleman bowing and paying his respects to them. Caleb recognised him as the son of one of their rival furniture businesses, Birneys. He and Mr. Swann had met him at conferences, and he had been invariably cold to Caleb, never speaking to him and responding only in monosyllables. Caleb thought he was being snobbish.

When Mr. Birney Jr kissed Stella's hand and then placed his own hand upon hers, lingering for some moments, something awakened in Caleb.

He's not being cold to me because I'm not cut from the cloth—he's cold because he loves Stella!

The revelation did not disturb him, and he felt disturbed because he felt no jealousy as Mr. Birney Jr fell into step beside his fiancée and her mother. How did Stella feel about Mr. Birney?

Harvey was not finished with his rival. He sidled up to him and smirked.

"You saw what I saw, did you not? You have a rival! Your goose is cooked." Harvey went away chuckling to himself.

I must ask her, Caleb thought to himself. *I can't end the engagement, it's not right. She must.*

He waited until a week into December and then asked her to go for a walk with him. She slipped her arm into his.

She liked to be seen with him; they received looks of admiration.

"Stella, I must ask you your intentions. We've been engaged a long time now. Is your heart still in it?"

"Caleb, how can you ask? Of course it is!"

"So this man Birney, he means nothing to you?"

"Oh, you saw that, did you? He is a sweet man but you're superior to him in looks and in temper, but he is from a very good family, superior to mine. And you're Papa's protege. No, I prefer you to him. I thought you knew that, Caleb."

"Of course, I just wanted to be sure," he said. "If you wished to be free, Stella, I would honour your wish. I think he loves you."

"I know he does—he told me so."

"He told you?"

"Yes, while you were at Hetherton summer last."

"And you gave him a definite no?"

"Oh, of course!"

Caleb wondered about this. Would a rejected man be so forward as to kiss the beloved's hand and cover it with his own? Not unless he had some little bit of encouragement, he thought.

He was quiet and felt resigned. They would not be unhappy together. It was something he often said to himself.

"Mama and I depend upon you so much," Stella added, as if reading his thoughts. "And do not forget your masterpiece, you must work on it quickly!"

He had already begun the furniture that he would present to the other Masters, so that he too could be called a Master. He designed a dressing table with intricate carvings as decoration and curved drawers with brass knobs, and so far, had completed most of the parts in the workshop.

THE MASTERPIECE

Christmas was approaching again. Preparations were being made in the Grace household. Babs knew that there would be no excursion to Swanns Furniture in Whitechapel this Christmas Eve. There was no reason—no excuse—to go there.

Mrs. Grace had introduced her to a young gentleman who was the cousin of a distant friend. He paid Babs attention but it was of the empty, flirtatious kind. For her part, she tried to like Mr. Elliott mainly because Mrs. Grace wished her to. Mrs. Grace was going to the North for two years, to see if she liked it there near her sister. She would not require a companion, so her job was coming to an end as soon as the winter ended.

Mrs. Grace hoped that Mr. Elliott would propose marriage to her companion and absolve her of any further worry about her future. She could go north with an easy mind. She wondered how his intentions lay, and on one occasion when he was visiting, she asked him. His response took her by surprise and displeased her, for she was an incurable romantic and had arranged everything in her own mind.

"Mrs. Grace," he said with an earnest and very serious expression. "I find myself surprised that you should think I had any intentions of the sort toward Miss Wren. She's not at all the sort of wife I would think of. Oh, she is pretty enough, that she is, but who is she? Where are her family? As to fortune—she has nothing! I am mortified that my polite attentions may have given rise to expectations. I hope she is not too disappointed, but I believe myself very innocent in the matter. Now if you will excuse me, I have an appointment with a colleague—we are going to Lady Wilmington's 'at home' party."

Mr. Elliott skedaddled as fast as he could, and was never seen again, and Mrs. Grace was very deflated. She confided in Babs, and Babs laughed and said she thought that she had 'a narrow escape' from a snob like Mr. Elliott.

"Please do not worry about me," she told her. "I will get another job as a companion, with the good reference you will give me!"

Babs put an advertisement in the newspaper and got one promising response from an elderly matron who wished to be accompanied to Bath for her health in the spring and wished to get to know her companion before they undertook the journey.

"I know Mrs. Hackett. She's a fussy old lady and you'll be at her beck and call," Mrs Debbie Delamere said when she visited next. It seemed she knew everybody. "But Bath is a good place to meet people! Yes, take it!"

"But—until then?"

"Stay with me!" Mrs. Delamere said.

Mrs. Delamere still mulled over the Mr. Dalton situation, she was sure that no marriage had taken place and that Miss Swann had been warned of his wicked nature. Possessed of a very curious nature herself and with little to do with her time, she decided to investigate.

She dressed up one day in jewellery and furs and made her way to Swanns Furniture Showrooms, pretending to be interested in a purchase. There, she observed a man she was sure must be Mr. Dalton. He looked surly and dissatisfied with the world, was directing prospective buyers towards the furniture they requested in an offhand sort of way, and taking no more interest in them after that, so that when they saw they were getting no more attention, they left.

She approached him. "My good man, I take it you work here? Are you Mr. Dalton?"

"No, Madam," he snapped.

She smelled alcohol on his breath. "Mr Dalton is up there in the Director's office, which is where *I* ought to be."

This was very interesting to the lady.

"Are you of the family, then?"

"I am Mrs. Swann's nephew, but the old man Swann would not give me the time of day. I come in here simply to annoy Mr. Dalton. He can't stop me being here."

"Perhaps you are doing your best to drive customers away?"

"I hope so."

"There must be some redress for yourself," she said to him, sympathetic that Mr. Dalton had pushed his way in ahead of the nephew.

"The only redress, Madam, is something I cannot speak of, though I am well on the way to it. But—if I cannot have it, nobody shall have it. He will know his place. He will end up with nothing, and he will never marry Miss Swann." His glazed eyes were full of something that alarmed her, and she took a step backwards.

"I was under the impression that they were married!" she exclaimed, excited at the new information.

"Oh, not they! Miss Swann is becoming wise to him. Her interest now lies *elsewhere*."

It was as she suspected then! But it would not be just to dear little Babs to encourage a marriage between her and Mr. Dalton, no matter what Phoebe Grace thought, for Phoebe herself was blind when it came to romance and her one view of Mr. Dalton had made him into a man like her dear departed Maurice.

"Did you come here to look at furniture?" he swayed a little, and she, becoming a little frightened of him, decided to go toward the door.

"I have just now recalled an urgent matter; I must leave."

"You may not get another chance!" he shouted after her, before collapsing in a chair with drunken laughter.

"What is the commotion, Vernon?" Dalton had come out of his office and was looking down at him from the balcony above.

Ah! This was Mr. Dalton! She looked up to see him. He was nice-looking.

"Wait until you see the commotion," he said to her with glee. He dropped his voice then: "You will read about it in the *Times* tomorrow perhaps."

"May I help you, Madam?" Mr. Dalton asked, coming swiftly down the stairs.

"I'm afraid I will have to leave it until another time," she said.

Mr. Dalton opened the door for her, and she had a good look at him. She saw an openness and honesty in his eyes, unlike the other, who was now slouching in a chair, scratching a polished table top with his penknife.

"STOP!" Caleb ordered him, as soon as the door shut behind the customer. He tried to snatch the knife from Harvey's hand, but Harvey was too quick for him, and got to his feet, brandishing the knife.

"Get out," Caleb said. Harvey looked at him, and at the knife, and slid it into his pocket as he sauntered into the workshop.

Caleb looked at him, wanting to throw him out for good, but it would be no use—his aunt would allow him back in.

If I could just get my masterpiece done, Caleb thought to himself, *I would go away from here. I've given Stella enough time to call it off—we know we aren't right for each other—she has her eye on Birney and I—I want to go home. I will stay late tonight and work on my masterpiece again.*

VERNON'S REVENGE!

~~~

He stayed late after work. It was misting outside. The large workshop was dark and he had one lamp burning to see what he was doing. There was nobody else there, and he was completely absorbed rummaging through the box of little brass knobs for the rose-shaped ones he knew would be an attractive finishing touch that a lady would admire.

He did not see or hear Harvey come in the back door that led to the yard. He did not see Harvey pause and look at him. He did not see what he carried—a tin of flammable oil. He did not see or hear him pour it, but the smell of the oil reached his nostrils, and he frowned. Then he heard a match strike.

He looked up suddenly to hear a loud noise and saw a large flame rise from where the sawdust and woodchips were against the wall. In the sudden light he saw a man—

the man who had surely caused the fire, for he was now a part of the blaze. A loud and desperate scream rose from the fiery silhouette.

Caleb rushed to him, shouting 'Fire! Fire!' He took the only thing he could lay hands on to help—his own greatcoat, and covered the screaming man with it, knocking him away from the flames and toward the door. As he did, a sheet of flame met him in the face and he cried out also, instinctively putting his arms up to protect himself.

Two men who had been working in the boneyard rushed in and rescued them, putting out the flames that threatened to engulf Caleb with damp canvas sacks, and dragging both men out into the rain.

Nothing could save Swanns Furniture Factory, the pride and joy of the lowly tradesman who had died only a short time before. The flames rushed through it, greedy for all the wood—the workroom was ravaged first, the offices, then the elegant showrooms. Six or seven young men rushed in and saved some furniture—not for the rightful owners, but for themselves to sell. They were a gang of thieves. Whitechapel was an area rising in crime.

The Metropolitan Fire Brigade arrived and there was a great commotion as the firemen rushed to stop it spreading to the houses nearby.

Caleb and Harvey were carried to the Swann's home where a hysterical household awaited them. Caleb was laid upon the table in the servants' hall, his shirt cut off by Mrs. Barnes the housekeeper, and streams of cold water applied to his red, blistered face and eyes. He groaned and moaned from the burning, scorching pain, followed by the cold stream which seemed to hurt as much as the fire, but Mrs. Barnes was adamant that cold water would save him, and she kept asking for more from the cook who was busy helping her. Stella stood at the door, terrified at the change she could already see in Caleb's appearance.

"My hands, my hands!" Caleb held them up in front of him, but he could not see them through his closed, burnt eyes.

"Water on his hands!" the housekeeper ordered. She looked toward the door, calling "Miss Swann! Come and assist!" but Stella withdrew. She fled upstairs. The kitchenmaid responded instead.

Mrs. Swann was in the drawing room with her maid Jennings and the parlourmaid, kneeling and weeping beside her dying nephew who had been placed upon the sofa. He rasped from the burning in his throat. She knew it was hopeless. She put a wooden cross in his hands. He looked at it, kissed it with his blistered lips, and died shortly after.

"May God have mercy on him," she cried aloud. "Poor orphan boy, poor bitter child!"

RECOVERY

The following morning, Babs arose in Mrs. Delamere's home. It was not long before news of the big fire in Whitechapel reached them.

"Oh mercy! It was at Swann's furniture! It's ruined!" said Mrs. Delamere when her manservant brought her the newspaper at breakfast. "It's gone completely! One man died! Another severely injured!"

Babs jumped up from her seat to look over her shoulder. "It doesn't say who is dead! Oh, I pray it's not Mr. Dalton! Not that I want anybody to die, but I pray it's not him!"

"It says that the man who was responsible for the fire is the man who died," Mrs. Delamere said. "And I know who that was—for I was there only yesterday and met him! He threatened Mr. Dalton!"

"You were there yesterday! Why?"

"I wished to find out something—something important, and I did—Mr. Dalton is still a bachelor and Miss Swann's eyes are wandering. There! But the man I met was a dreadful man, in his cups and vengeful, and he said that Dalton would be sorry because he was taking his place there, his rightful place, he called it, I think. I thought Dalton must be a cad but having met both, I think Dalton must be the better of the two."

"But who is the injured man? I pray it's not Mr. Dalton!"

"The newspaper does not say. Why are you looking at me like that, child?"

"I am going to set out for there this morning," she said.

Mrs. Delamere was delighted. "I shall order the carriage and we'll be on our way after breakfast. "Mrs. Delamere was as keen as Babs to see the excitement, for that is what it was for her.

"Everybody loves a fire," she said with enthusiasm, before backtracking into: "But only if there is no loss of life of course! And no injuries! And not much loss of property, and the property is well insured. Then everyone loves a fire, for to see those brave men fighting it, and running up and down ladders rescuing people, throwing hysterical ladies in their nightgowns over their shoulders as if they weighed nothing at all, is admirable! A great offense against modesty, of course, but nobody minds in the circumstances."

She was speaking to herself, for Babs had run off to get her mantle and bonnet. She called for the carriage, and they set off.

Whitechapel was congested this morning.

"I smell smoke," Babs said uneasily as they approached Ferry Street. She fidgeted. Was Caleb all right? Was he the injured man? Was the fire out? They alighted the carriage and walked into the street, and joined a crowd of people who were there, from all walks of life, looking at the ruins of what had been promising to be one of the most prestigious furniture shops in London. It was a sad, charred shell. The roof had fallen in. It had an eerie silence. Only a few pieces of furniture had survived the torching and the looting, and even they would be no good to sell. There were some men inside, gingerly poking their way here and there. Caleb was not one of them.

"I pray you tell me, where does the family live?" Babs asked a constable in an agitated manner. They might have to take another carriage ride to there.

But the constable pointed out a house just next door. "The Swanns live there," he said. "They're in mourning, don't knock on the door."

"We heard that a man was injured," Mrs Delamere said. "Who was that?"

"He is a Mr. Dalton. He was an apprentice I think."

Babs drew in a sharp breath. "Oh, is he badly injured? I hope he is not bad!" she exclaimed, while Mrs. Delamere put an arm about her. "Oh, I pray he will be all right! Constable, may we not enquire?"

"I suppose that if you are friends of his family, it will be all right," he said, before shouting at one of the men in the ruins that he was about to enter a dangerous area.

They went to the door and the housekeeper answered.

"May I enquire who you are?"

"I am Mrs. Delamere and I was in the showroom yesterday, and I feel dreadful for what has happened—I wished to return and ask for Mr. Dalton."

"That is very kind of you, Mrs. Delamere. He is in fair condition; his eyes are burned

and—" Babs had allowed a fearful cry to escape her, so she stopped.

"May I see him, please?" she begged. "We are acquainted."

Mrs Barnes, who had been up all night and only that morning had witnessed a distressing scene between Mrs. Swann and her daughter, was touched that a sweet young lady, her large dark eyes filled with tears, cared for Mr. Dalton. Because Miss Swann had left the house that morning to go and stay with her mother's sister in Kensington and had no intention of returning.

She went to inform Mrs. Swann, who came downstairs.

"You are acquainted!" she said. "How?"

Babs's eyes filled with tears again. All she could say was: "He saved my life on Christmas Eve nearly three years ago! I was—"

"You are that young lady!" Mrs. Swann said. "Pray what is your name?"

"I'm Miss White," Babs said.

Mrs. Delamere had no idea what Babs was talking of; Phoebe had never told her all this! This was intriguing indeed! She congratulated herself for being in the thick of a mystery. And if Miss Wren was calling herself Miss White, she would go along with that too.

They entered the hallway and followed Mrs. Swann upstairs.

"I am very, *very* glad to see you, Miss White." she said, turning about unexpectedly. Mrs. Delamere's eyes widened. What was all this? It was turning out to be better than any serial in a periodical! Except that someone died of course, and someone else injured—but not too badly, she hoped.

They went on, but Mrs. Swann paused outside the room. "I do not know how to say this," she said rather awkwardly. "Up to this morning, my daughter was engaged to Mr. Dalton. But she has gone. The engagement is over." She seemed to be addressing Babs.

"Perhaps it was just the shock," Mrs. Delamere said, fishing for more information. "She will be back in a few days, and all will be well between them."

"No, she will not." Mrs. Swann sounded very sure, and Mrs. Delamere gave Babs an encouraging nudge and a wink as the door opened.

"Caleb, there is a Miss White to see you."

The room was in semi-darkness. Caleb was sitting up in the four-poster bed, his eyes bandaged, his hands on the counterpane, bandaged also. There was a nurse folding bandages by a table.

"Miss White? Miss Anne White?" Caleb stirred and turned his head toward her.

"Anne White," said Babs, going to him, lightly touching his arm. She could not help it—he could not see her, and she wanted him to feel her touch, if he could not see her. Besides, had she not known this man for as long as she could remember?

Anne White, Mrs. Delamere repeated to herself, lest she make a mistake.

"I came to you as soon as I heard about the fire, Mr. Dalton," Babs said. She kept her hand on his forearm.

"That was very kind of you," he said. His lips were blistered and his cheeks red and inflamed.

"It was as much as I could do, considering what you did for me," she said. "I would not be alive were it not for your great kindness to me."

He smiled a little. "You were in a bad way, and it's my happiness that you've recovered."

Mrs. Swann motioned Mrs. Delamere to leave the room with her, and the latter very reluctantly obeyed.

"It will be my happiness when you recover," Babs said.

"I will recover, then. Will you sit by me for a little while and talk to me?"

But the nurse would not allow it. "Mr. Dalton, the doctor said you are to rest. He gave you a sedative." She turned a stern eye on Babs.

"Is it too much of me to ask you to come back to see me again?" Caleb asked.

"No, it is not too much. I would like to see you very much." But Babs was weeping, and he detected it and looked toward her, though he could not see her. "I'm sorry," she said. "I know you're a craftsman, and you must get better, for you need your eyes and your hands."

"I will get better," he said.

She put her hand on his head. "I'm praying for you," she said, weeping again.

"Do not upset the patient," the nurse said sternly, for she suspected that Mr. Dalton was becoming emotional and that would be very bad for him indeed. *Peace and Quiet* was what the doctor said.

Downstairs, Babs found Mrs. Delamere and Mrs. Swann drinking tea and talking together.

"My husband and my nephew dead within a short time of each other, and Caleb like this. If Miss White would visit him often, I would be ever so grateful, for I cannot sit by him; I feel unable for it, and now he is not to be part of the family… my daughter could not bear his looks, could not bear to see him without his health and his strength, and so she left. But—she did not love him after all. Not for a moment did I ever think Caleb was a fortune hunter, though some say it looked like that…I want to make sure he will be set up in life, after what my nephew tried to do to him."

Mrs. Delamere drank it all up with three cups of sweet tea.

"Miss White loves him," she said frankly, knowing she was advancing the cause of Babs Wren, alias Miss White. She could not wait to get Babs alone to get it all out of her.

"I am glad of that. My sister sent a note telling me to send Caleb to a hospital, with all that is on my hands at the moment, but I do not want to do that, for he served my husband very well for these last seven years, and he deserves to be looked after here, in this place which has been his home…the doctor said his injuries are not very bad, and that the quick service the housekeeper rendered to him may have gone a long way toward saving his sight and his hands. Now here is Miss White, have a cup of tea, my dear. You will come often, won't you?"

They left soon after and by the time they had reached home Mrs. Delamere was apprised of all the details of Christmas Eve nearly three years ago and what had gone before, in Hetherton, Essex. What a story!

"I beg you to keep it to yourself," Babs asked. Mrs. Delamere promised that she would, at least until they were married, and that, she supposed, could not be far away.

"I think you should tell him who you are," Mrs Delamere advised. "But ask permission of the nurse, for I understand the doctor doesn't want any surprises, and this my dear Babs, would be a big surprise."

"And I don't want to tell him while she's there; it would spoil it!" she said. "She's strict and formal, and it would spoil everything if she interfered and shooed me away."

Babs had to wait, but in the meantime, there were certain things she could find out.

"Mrs. Swann, has Mr. Dalton's family been informed about him?" she asked the following morning on her way up the stairs.

"Yes—he dictated a letter and it was sent."

"So—will they come to see him?"

"Oh, no. He doubts it. He wrote that he was only slightly injured, but was anxious they know about the fire because it was very likely the vicar or the schoolmaster would have seen it in the paper and told them. His parents—do not take the newspaper. In any case, his mother and father never travel, and his sister is too near her time to think of undertaking a journey."

"Near her time!" Babs just stopped herself in time from exclaiming: 'Alice! You're speaking of my dearest friend Alice!'

"Yes," Mrs. Swann mistook Babs's surprise for naïveté. "She will be confined of a child very soon," she explained.

Alice was having a baby! Her heart danced with excitement. Alice must be married, then! Oh, who did Alice marry! An old schoolmate, one of the Tarrant boys perhaps? Or was it Jim Bates who she was sweet on for a time? How she longed to see Alice and find out everything about her romance! Her heart suddenly longed for Hetherton.

THE REVELATION

Caleb was very impatient to get out of bed and he soon quarrelled with Nurse Evans. They compromised; he could sit out for meals.

The bandages were removed from his hands after a week, and the doctor was very pleased that they were healing well.

"It's your youth," he said cheerfully. "Now, Miss White, what say *you*?"

"I thank God they are all right! He's a cabinet maker, you know."

"Yes, I know! I say, young man, I was sorry to hear that your masterpiece is in ashes. No doubt it would have been a beautiful object."

"Yes, it's unfortunate," Caleb said. "Miss White, I was making a dressing table for a lady's bedchamber; it was nearly finished. It would have entitled me to be called 'Master' of my trade."

"You shall make another, Mr. Dalton! How long before the bandages can come off the eyes, doctor?"

"Another few days. Christmas Eve. What, have I said something?" For a smile had passed between the two sweethearts, a private smile. Though his patient was blindfolded, he knew exactly where Miss White stood in relation to him and directed his smile in her direction.

"Nothing, Doctor." Caleb said. "Except it is a special time, of course."

After he left, the nurse was absent from the room for a few minutes, gone to the kitchen to give orders for a nourishing chicken soup for the patient's supper. Babs took the opportunity.

"If your bandages come off on Christmas Eve, can you make your way to the usual place?"

"Of course I can. I don't mind what Dragon Nurse says; I'm bigger than her."

"I have a surprise for you," she said.

"What is that? I can hardly wait!"

"Oh, you must wait! You told me I reminded you of someone."

"Yes! Is that it? Who are you? I have gone over everybody I know in this city and beyond…"

"Wait until Christmas Eve! But may we meet in daylight? It is dark at five, and I want to be alone, not accompanied by Mrs. Delamere. I heard her say she has calls to make on Christmas Eve morning, so shall we say eleven o'clock?" She caressed his hands softly. "Does that hurt?"

"No, not at all. Do they look all right? Are they red or blistered or anything?"

"They're just a little pinkish on the fingertips."

"Press on my fingertips—go on, don' be afraid—only don't tell me which finger—that was my middle finger right hand, wasn't it?"

"Yes!"

"Try them all."

She did so. He felt every touch, identified it correctly, and was elated. "I will work again. I will begin on another masterpiece as soon as I can. Swanns was insured, and Mrs. Swann said that she wishes me to have capital to start me off on my own. It will be a small beginning, but I know I can work again."

"Do you know, dear," said Mrs. Delamere later, "I am sure you will not take this situation with Mrs. Greyhurst to go to Bath. I've taken the liberty of informing her that you won't go."

"Mrs Delamere! Why did you do so?"

"Because you are not going, and she will need to find another person."

Babs thought it high-handed but considered that Mrs. Delamere could be right. She and Caleb were in love. They did not need to speak the words—but what if he rejected her when he found out she was little Miss Ugly Duckling Wren? *Don't be silly*, she told herself.

Caleb might help her to look for Pip! He'd been in London for seven years; he would know where to look. How she longed to see him again, to know that he was all right, in a steady job, and perhaps had a sweetheart?

Mrs. Delamere wanted to know. "Because I wish to call on some friends in the morning to wish them a Merry Christmas. Will you come with me? No? That is a very definite shake of the head. How will you get to Whitechapel? By cab. I see. Very well, Miss Independent. I shouldn't allow you to go without a chaperone, but—I will have to take the chance."

Babs felt giddy for the rest of the day. She brushed her hair with one hundred strokes that night and worried if a tiny red mark on her chin was developing into a pimple. She worried about falling asleep and that if she did not get any sleep that she would look wretched in the morning.

She wore her red mantle and the ivory-trimmed bonnet. She could only get a cab part of the way, so she walked the rest. She came upon Ferry Street about eleven o'clock, and Caleb was there, standing beside the ruined frontage, his bandages were gone, his eyes clear but for a little irritation around both of them and down his cheek.

"It healed very well," she said to him.

He shook his head. "I'm grateful I won't be blind—so grateful!" He turned to the ruined shopfront, the crumbling, charred walls, the windows now boarded up.

"It's the first time I've laid eyes on it since the fire," he said. He contemplated it for a moment, remarked 'Seven years' and turned to her. "I will have a scar or two. Do you think it will be awful for anyone to look at?"

"No, not at all, Caleb."

"You called me Caleb, we were on first-name terms then? Were we? It must have been a long time ago!" He had a little questioning smile.

Now that the time had come to reveal herself, she became tongue-tied. She rushed into a wall of shyness, and was hardly able to speak.

"Miss—White? Who are you?" he asked.

"Do you remember," she said suddenly. "Do you remember one day—in the downs at Hetherton—a flock of sheep—and a flock of starlings—and a sparrowhawk—and the birds hid among the sheep on the grass? Who was in the field with you, that day?"

"It was Babs Wren," he said wonderingly, but nothing seemed to register in his eyes. Then his face grew pale as he scrutinised her. "You can't be—but you can't be Babs! Babs Wren!"

"Yes, that is me! That is me! All grown up, not a child anymore! What's the matter? Do I look so altered? Why are you so shocked?" For she thought that he was looking at her with disbelief and dread—his face had paled so much! A familiar feeling sprouted in her heart. *Is this Christmas Eve going to bring heartbreak to me as well? He is agitated and looks as if he does not want to know me! He will reject me! Oh, what is this?*

But the explanation came tumbling from his lips, probably because he saw her lip tremble and her eyes fall to her feet in confusion. He put his hands on her shoulders.

"But—you would be shocked too if you thought you were seeing a ghost! We thought you dead—You did come into my mind when I was searching for the girls I knew, but when I was in Hetherton some time ago, I was told that you had died of a fever and were no more. I was very sorry to hear of it, for I had always been fond of you. So I thought, *well Miss White cannot be Babs Wren—though I would love her to be Babs Wren!*"

It was a shock to Babs to find out she was supposed to be dead.

"I'm here and very much alive," she said. "I don't know how that story got about. So, Alice thinks I'm dead too?

Oh no! Everybody thinks I'm dead?" She was distressed, so he took her in his arms.

"We have to remedy this as soon as we can. I'm going to Hetherton this evening." he said. "Will you come with me? Please?"

"Who did Alice marry?" she asked eagerly, the question burning on her heart ever since she had heard the news.

"Alice is Mrs. Philip Wren and they live in Hetherton with my parents."

"Pip! Our Pip! Oh Caleb, you are not joking me, I hope! Can it be true?"

"Oh my, more tears to be kissed away" he said, putting it into action.

"Joy! My brother is found, my brother is safe. We lost each other here in London—it's a very long story, Caleb!"

"I have more news—your brother Geoff came back from America. He didn't like it there. He's in Essex as well! Come, let's go and get your things from Mrs. Delamerey or whatever her name is, and we'll set out tonight. Oh, to make it all proper so there's no talk of chaperones—will you marry me, Miss Wren?"

"Yes, yes, Caleb Dalton, I'll marry you!"

An old man passing by said to his companion: "It looks like snow, it does! A white Christmas, eh?"

RETURN TO HETHERTON

Mrs. Delamere was not at all surprised to see the couple waiting for her in the drawing room when she returned from making her calls. She complimented Caleb on his looking well and the news of their engagement did not surprise her either.

"So, you are going today—get to the railway station directly after lunch, for it will snow. I will miss you at Christmas, dear, but luckily Miss Boone and her mother are coming for dinner."

Caleb had an urgent errand at the post office, so after that he was free to do as he pleased. It was beginning to snow as they made their way to Liverpool Street. It was thronged—the weather had moved everybody's plans forward.

"I can't believe I'm on my way back to Essex," Babs said more than once, looking out the window at the passing fields now being gently stroked in white by the steady snowfall. The train was full of happy country folk going home for Christmas. Many got out at Chelmsford, and as the train steamed towards Hetherton, Babs could hardly contain her excitement.

"Look!" HETHERTON was painted in large letters as the train pulled into the station.

It was getting dark, but lights twinkled in the cottages and homes. Caleb carried a lamp obtained at the railway station. Some of the shops were still open and the welcome smell of gingerbread came from the baker's. They came to the church; flickering golden light was visible through the lancet windows and Christmas carols were in their hearing, for the choir was rehearsing. Babs stopped to take in the scene, to look and to listen. All was white around them and the snowflakes fell silently.

"Let's go in for a minute," she said.

They lingered at the back of the church.

"That's the Austrian carol. I heard it at my brother Henry's! It's been translated to English."

Silent Night, Holy Night

All is calm, all is bright

Round yon Virgin Mother and Child

Holy Infant so tender and mild

Sleep in Heavenly Peace,

Sleep in Heavenly Peace.

Babs felt peace settle upon her heart. Pip was safe. Caleb loved her. She was home. Surely Christmas was a time of peace and grace and gentleness and restoration and love, if only mankind would see it that way! The vicar saw them and came down the church. He was astounded to find that Babs Wren was before him, very much alive! He said that he would announce it to the congregation on the morrow before service began, to save everybody the speculation of wondering, for it would be a great distraction.

"Welcome home, Babs," he said to her, shaking her hand and going up the church again.

"We had best get on, love," Caleb said, nudging her.

"Are they expecting you?" Babs asked.

"Yes, I told them some time ago that I'd be home for Christmas, and I sent a telegram that you were alive so they don't all faint in front of our eyes."

"I wonder how Alice is! I can't wait to see her and Pip!"

A labouring man crunching along the ground greeted Caleb: *'Chippy Dalton! Merry Christmas to you and yours!'* and looked strangely at the girl with him, so that she determined to keep her head low. After all, she was supposed to be *dead,* and she did not want to frighten anybody on Christmas Eve by making them think they had seen a ghost. Everybody would know tomorrow, on Christmas Day.

She looked up at Redgate House. The downstairs windows were lit, and her old room upstairs.

"When I was a little girl, Caleb, I used to look out that window and imagine that your hill—Hetherton Hill—was filled with heavenly lights and angels singing."

"Why Hetherton Hill?"

"Because of you being shepherds, of course! I felt that shepherds must be special to God."

"I suppose we are, in a way," he said. "For we are in the Good Book a lot, aren't we?"

"And Jesus is the Good Shepherd who cares for His flock and looks for the lost sheep."

"Who lives at Redgate now?" she asked after a moment of contemplating the above.

"A family named Crooks. Good people."

"Where are we going now? This isn't the way to your house."

"We have to make a call here first." He steered her towards a laneway that she remembered had at the very end of it a cottage in which old Mo lived; Old Mo who used to play the accordion for the dances on the green. A dog began to bark as they advanced; Caleb holding the lamp aloft.

"Why are we calling upon Old Mo?"

"We're not. Old Mo's been dead these two years."

"Who are we calling upon then?"

"People you know."

"It must be Geoff! He lives here, does he?" But he did not make any reply.

The windows were brightly lit and there was a red candle flickering in one of them.

They knocked, and the door opened. There was a middle-aged woman there, with a face dear and familiar, and smiling, her arms out to embrace her.

"My dear Barbara!"

"Mama! Is it really you? You came back! Oh, thank God!" They embraced warmly, and Babs had copious tears again.

There was great excitement then, for the old familiar step of her father was heard and he came too and wrapped his daughter in his arms. Then Geoff appeared and Babs rushed to him.

"Little sister, you've grown." He said, beaming, giving her a big hug. "*Howdy Chippy!*" he said to Caleb, putting on an

American accent. They shook hands. "Caleb, when we got your telegram today saying Babs was alive, we were overwhelmed with joy," Mrs. Wren said, clutching his arm as if she never wanted to let go of him. Thank you for bringing her home to us."

"But where did you go that night?" Babs asked them. "Henry wouldn't tell us anything." There was a little plaintiveness to her tone.

Mrs. Wren put the kettle on the fire and gathered cups and saucers and plates from the dresser, and signalled Babs to come and help her and out of direct earshot of the men who were chatting together, she said:

"Your father became very ill, Babs. He lost his mind. He ran from the house, thinking he would be arrested. I had to follow him, for I thought he was about to take his own life. I caught up with him. He would not come back with me, for he said that the cottage was surrounded by the Militia. We spent the night sheltering in a shepherd's hut, and at dawn I got him to Dr. Parry's house, and he said he had to be admitted to—a lunatic asylum. The asylum was in Chelmsford. I went with him. I was allowed to stay with him to nurse him in exchange for cooking for the staff. He was very ill, malnourished in body, delusional in his mind. I wrote to Henry to tell him to look after all of you. I told him *not* to tell you—for if it got out, your father would never be able to work again, your brothers might not be employed, and you might not get a husband. I could not contact you. It was better you did not know about this, but go and make lives for yourselves."

"So what did you tell them here in the village?"

"That he was at a sanitorium and is now cured."

The kettle was singing merrily on the fire, its lid lifting with the rolling boil.

"What's keeping the tea?" Mr. Wren shouted to them.

"Nothing dear, we will be ready in a moment," Mrs. Wren called back.

"You may be angry with me, Babs. I thought Henry would look after all of you. He sent Geoff to America, and it seems you and Pip left him, and got separated—you will have to tell me all about it, but not now, your father wants his tea...make it, dear, will you—three spoons." She handed her the tea caddy.

"Caleb and I are engaged, Mama! That is, if Papa gives his consent, of course." She lifted the kettle from the flames, removed the lid carefully and poured three spoons of tea leaves in, giving her father a smile.

"I do," said her father, pleased.

"You've saved me preparing my little speech, sir." Caleb said, smiling.

Tea was served with jollity, and fresh mince pies and a

little dab of cream. A little while later the door burst open and Pip was in their midst, his coat covered in snow.

"Is she here? Is Babs here?"

It was a very happy reunion between brother and sister, and many tears were shed. But after only a short time, Pip said: "I have to go now, it's snowing hard, and Alice—her time is very near, Ma says."

"You had better go too, before it gets too bad!" Mrs. Wren said to her future son-in-law. "We'll look the other way if you two lovebirds want to say goodnight."

A long quiet minute later, Mr. Wren said: "Well come on now. You'll see each other tomorrow! Say goodnight and be done!"

There was a giggle all around, and a gust of cold came in through the open door, and the whirling snowflakes enveloped the two men as they hurried home.

Her father looked tired but peaceful as he finished his tea and pushed his cup and saucer back from him, as was his lifelong habit.

"We have a goose for tomorrow," he said. "Look at it over there! A fine, plump goose! The Daltons are going to come and help us eat it."

"If Alice has her child tomorrow, we will take it up there, and we shall all sit around Caleb's beautiful rosewood table," Mrs. Wren said. "Babs, the cottage has been greatly improved! When Mr. Withers heard that they had been sent a fine table and we had no room for it, he was put to shame, and wouldn't have it said his head-shepherd was living in such a small poor cottage. So he widened it and added a good roof! Now it doesn't lose the heat like it used to, nor does the rain come through."

"I've never seen anything Caleb made, so I can't wait to see it," Babs said. "So we might eat there tomorrow? I hope so! Where did you get the goose?"

"Henry sent it with a nice little note," Mrs. Wren said, producing an envelope. "here, read it."

Dear Mother and Father and Brothers, I write somewhat ashamed of my neglect of you all these years. I hope to remedy this in the future. Please accept this present of a goose. We are all well. Albert is a fine little boy. He chatters a great deal. I will bring him to meet you when the weather's better. Or perhaps you would like to visit Whitholm again. Irene sends her fond regards. Your devoted son and brother, Henry.

It's a start, Babs thought, folding up the letter and placing it in the envelope. She did not want to remember how horrid he was to Pip and herself when they went to live there. It was Christmas and there was so much to be grateful for just now.

Mr. Wren turned in soon after that, then Geoff, and mother and daughter were alone to have a good chatter.

"I had to go to a workhouse for a time, Mama."

"That's dreadful! Do not ever disclose it! Not even to your father, for he feels bad enough about all that happened. No, that is another secret we must keep in the family. Did you bide there long?"

Babs told her all that had transpired. Then she asked: "How do you and Papa live, Mama?"

"Do you remember your father's business partner Mr Burlington? He has done well, and had pangs of conscience and has agreed to an annuity for your father. He should not have absconded as he did, leaving us with nothing but debt. But we will be all right, and Mr. Crooks up at Redgate needs an agent, for he has bought land."

"Did you mind, Mama, when you heard that Pip married Alice?"

"Oh no, Babs, I was very happy for him. Alice loves him and will make him a good wife. I'm not the snob I used to be, Babs! Nor is your father. We've been the recipients of the generosity of many people we used to look down upon—it's humbling. They have so little themselves and yet—they share. And you to marry Caleb—we couldn't be happier. Now we are all tired, I think it's time we went to bed."

A bed had been prepared and heated for her with a warming pan, and she slipped into it. The sheets were made of flour sacks and rough against her skin. She did not mind. She was home in Hetherton. Home with her mother and father, and only a quarter of a mile away her fiancé lived. She'd never leave Hetherton again, or if she did, it would only be to Chelmsford.

She dreamed that she was walking up the hill to the Dalton cottage, because she had not yet seen Alice. The snow was falling. Then there was bright light on the hillside, angels were singing, and all was Joy. The Dalton household was filled with exultation and happiness.

When she woke shortly after dawn, she wondered if her coming back to Hetherton had been a dream. But no, her mother and father were in their room sleeping, she heard Geoff snore in his, and when she looked out the window, her fiancé was approaching, coming quickly in his black greatcoat and muffler through the snow to see her. Around him every hillock and rooftop was covered in white.

She drew on her dressing gown, brushed her long dark hair quickly and opened the door to him. He came in and clasped her in his arms.

"Merry Christmas, Babs." he said. "I'm bringing happy news with me. I am an uncle and you are an aunt to an infant girl! She was born at five o'clock this morning. Mother and baby are well. Oh, what a perfect Christmas!"

The household had to be awakened then; all was rejoicing. They bundled up and walked to Church to celebrate the birth of Jesus, Our Saviour, and to give thanks for the safe delivery. A hot breakfast was eaten with relish, and later on dinner was prepared, and all brought up to Dalton's.

Alf and Dolly Dalton were very happy to see Babs and welcomed her as their future daughter-in-law. They had been thankful that Miss Swann was no longer in the picture, for they had suspected that all was not well there for a long time. They had been ecstatic that Babs was alive and well.

The cottage was improved indeed. It was larger and warmer. The rosewood table stood in the centre of the kitchen and was covered normally by an oilcloth to protect it, for it was more fit to grace a dining room, if there had been one. Today, however, it had a pretty green tablecloth and holly and ivy graced its centre.

"My first job will be to make rosewood chairs to match," Caleb said. "But come—you want to meet Alice!"

She was sitting up on the pillows, her sandy hair caught loosely into a white cap. The babe was in her arms. She had a soft fuzz of fair hair like her mother.

"I was getting tired last evening, and wondering if the babe would ever come, and when I 'eard Caleb's news that you was alive and well, I got fresh energy—all went well arter that, and the midwife was very pleased she had so little to do i' the end!"

As they chatted, the older women were setting the table and soon they were gathered around it. Alice was not supposed to get up, so a tray was brought to her, and she ate with relish. The others gathered around the fine table, and it was a very merry, happy party.

After the dishes had been cleared away and washed and more candles lit, Babs proposed they sing carols. Alice's door was left open so she could hear them as she lay on her pillows and cradled her newborn, and either Babs or Pip or Mrs. Dalton popped in to her every so often. They sang to their hearts' content, every carol they knew.

"It's time we went home," Mrs. Wren said about ten o'clock. But they were not allowed to leave without drinking a cup of hot tea for the 'journey.'

Caleb accompanied them. He and Babs walked in front of the older couple.

"That was the happiest Christmas I ever had!" Babs said contentedly. "It will leave a glow for me forever when I think back on it."

"Shall we name our wedding day?" he urged. "Let's not wait long!"

They decided on the last Sunday before Ash Wednesday.

THE END

Postscript

Caleb chose Chelmsford as a suitable place to begin business, and he rented a small house there to which to bring his bride and built a workshop beside it. Babs was a little disappointed that her home would not be the village she grew up in but knew that the growing town was a good spot to start a business, and it was not far away. They were married in February. The business thrived from the beginning and Caleb was very busy as he restarted his masterpiece. It was the same piece as before, a mahogany dressing table, elegant and practical. The masters approved it, and his parents were very proud. His father-in-law liked meeting customers and was often seen in the shop showing furniture to potential buyers. He came to live with them after Mrs Wren died, and by then they had four children. They purchased a larger home. Christmas was their favourite time of year and Babs made Christmas Day very special, and never lost sight of the Christ-Child as the season became more commercial and busier. They had a carol service in their drawing-room every Christmas Night, and the children continued this tradition in their own homes as they went away to make lives for themselves, married and had children. Their son Alfred was a cabinet maker and Dalton's Fine Furniture was well known by then.

Babs was very charitable and concerned for the poor. When her children were old enough, she confided to them that she had spent time in a workhouse. As her daughters tended to think themselves above others because their father was successful and they had a big house, this cured them. They decided to spend part of Christmas Day serving the workhouse poor. Babs and Caleb had a long marriage and lived to see their grandchildren marry.

Pip and Alice continued to live in Hetherton, and Pip rose to become land agent for Robert Withers with whom he used to play as a boy. Withers thought the slopes too good for sheep and sold the hill to a tillage farmer. By the turn of the century not a sheep or a lamb was left on Hetherton Hill, but Pip and Alice told their grandchildren stories of the old days when they were plentiful.

THANK YOU FOR CHOOSING A PUREREAD BOOK!

THANK YOU FOR CHOOSING A PUREREAD BOOK!

We hope you enjoyed the story, and as a way to thank you for choosing PureRead we'd like to send you this free book, and other fun reader rewards…

Click here for your free copy of Whitechapel Waif
PureRead.com/victorian

Thanks again for reading.
See you soon!

LOVE VICTORIAN CHRISTMAS SAGA ROMANCE?

If you enjoyed this story why not continue straight away with other books in our PureRead Victorian Christmas Romance library?

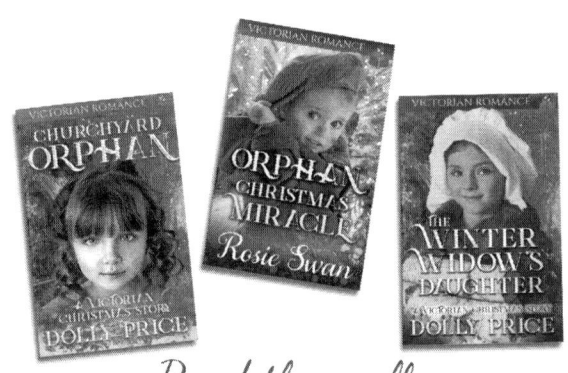

Read them all...

Churchyard Orphan

Orphan Christmas Miracle

Workhouse Girl's Christmas Dream

The Winter Widow's Daughter

The Match Girl & The Lost Boy's Christmas Hope

The Christmas Convent Child

The Orphan Girl's Winter Secret

Rag And Bone Winter Hope

Isadora's Christmas Plight

PLUS THESE DELIGHTFUL CHRISTMAS TALES
FROM OUR BESTSELLING VICTORIAN
ROMANCE AUTHORS

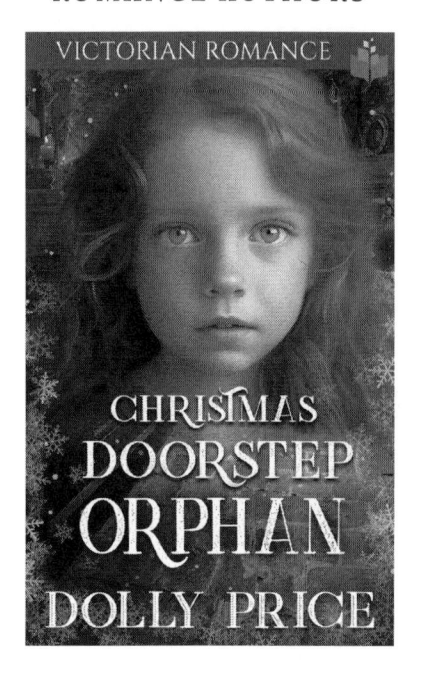

Read Christmas Doorstep Orphan on Amazon

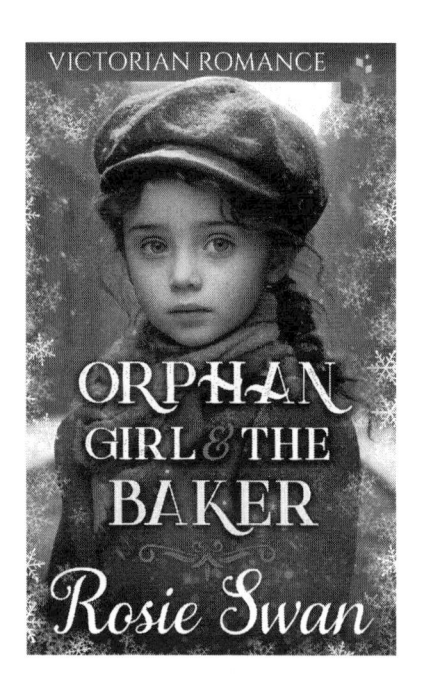

Read Orphan Girl & The Baker on Amazon

Read The Desperate Christmas Angel

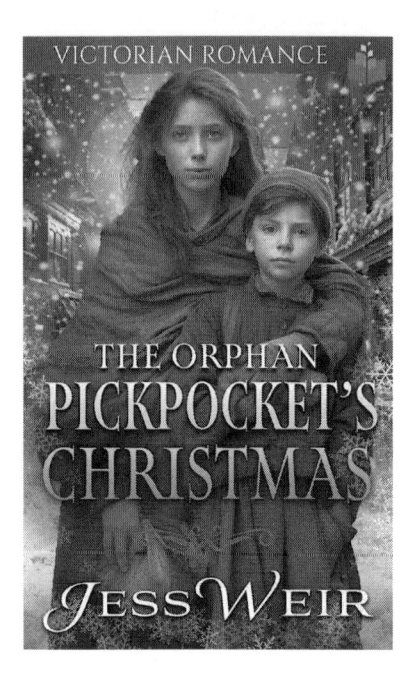

Read The Orphan Pickpocket's Christmas

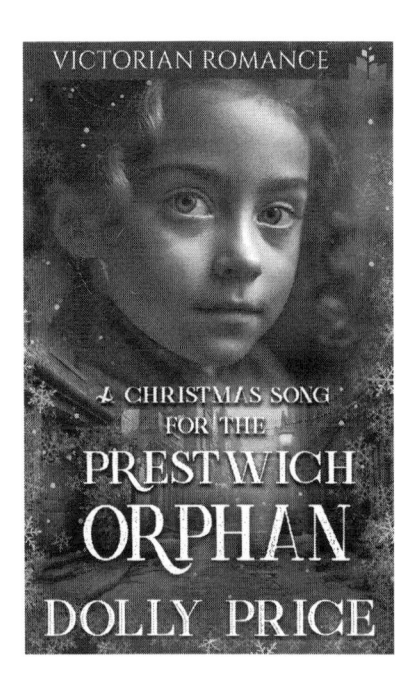

A Christmas Song For The Prestwich Orphan

HAVE YOU READ?

CHRISTMAS DOORSTEP ORPHAN

Now that you have experienced the wonder of 'A Shepherd's Son and The Lady' why not dive straight into another unputdownable Victorian Romance?

Keep warming your heart at the romance hearth with Dolly Price's bestselling *Christmas Doorstep Orphan*.

This story begins on a frosty Christmas Day. An unexpected arrival shakes the opulent world of the Leigh-Donner family in Belgravia. A mysterious note claims the abandoned child is their kin, but they're reluctant to embrace her as their own...

What will happen to little baby Emma?

You'll not be able to stop turning the pages of this warmhearted historical yuletide saga! 🤍

PS: Prepare to shed a few happy tears!

VICTORIAN ROMANCE

CHRISTMAS DOORSTEP ORPHAN

DOLLY PRICE

"Good morning, Colonel, and you, too, Madam. May I wish you both a very merry Christmas." The butler entered the breakfast room with a covered platter of hot sausages, bacon, eggs, smoked fish, and toast to serve the colonel and his lady personally, which he always did on special occasions.

"And we wish you the same, Perkins," replied his mistress. Her husband took the cover off the platter, and the delicious aroma of Christmas breakfast filled the room.

"There was a snowfall during the night," Mrs. Leigh-Donner said.

"It has begun again, Madam." Perkins looked toward the window, and their eyes followed his, just in time to see a carriage halt outside amid the whirling snowflakes.

"There is somebody out today," the colonel said. "It's too

early to be Charlotte and the children. The neighbours have visitors, I expect."

The doorbell rang, startling them. Who could be at their door on Christmas morning?

"Excuse me," Perkins said, setting the platter down and making for the door.

"Very odd," remarked Colonel Leigh-Donner.

They heard voices in animated debate in the hallway.

Perkins burst into the room, rather quickly for his usual gravitas.

"It is a policeman, Colonel, to see you and Mrs. Leigh-Donner, and he bears a -" he stopped, for the constable was upon his heels and had entered the room. In his arms was a small child covered in a blanket, a woolly cap about the head. The child was asleep.

There was amazement.

"What, is he injured? Lay him on the easy chair, and we will fetch a doctor." Mrs. Leigh-Donner assumed that there had been an accident outside their door.

"No, it is not that." Perkins was red-faced and very agitated. "The constable says there is a note come with her."

Trembling, he thrust a piece of paper into the colonel's

hands. There, he read, in bold capital letters, the following words.

MY NAME IS EMMA. I WAS BORN ON 1ST JULY 1859 IN A COUNTRY FAR AWAY. PLEASE TAKE ME TO MY PATERNAL GRANDPARENTS AT 11 ELIZABETH STREET, BELGRAVIA.

"Emma! My own name!" Mrs. Leigh-Donner fainted.

"She was found last night at Victoria Station in the ladies waiting room," said the constable. "She spent the night at the police station, wrapped up as warm as they could make 'er. Where shall I set the child?" He was getting impatient, for he wished to be rid of his burden, and he was forming the idea that the couple at this address had no wish to be acquainted with the child. It was a long way to a workhouse, and he had no wish to go there in a snowfall.

The housekeeper, Mrs. Breen, appeared then, and having been shown the note by Mr. Perkins, took the child from the constable, who made a hurried departure.

Assistance was found for her mistress, who was recovering. The colonel was stricken dumb.

"I shall take the child downstairs and give her milk," said Mrs. Breen. "What a shock!"

Mrs. Leigh-Donner was able to sip some hot coffee and managed a slice of toast and a little poached egg. The colonel ate a hearty breakfast. He always said that eating helped him to think, and not even a shock like this would cause him to neglect his Christmas breakfast.

"Grandparents indeed! She cannot be our family," Emma said flatly. "Our boys are good boys."

The colonel said nothing. He had been in the army a long time and knew that plenty of young men sowed their wild oats while their mothers at home thought them saints.

They had two living sons, and neither was in England. Wesley was in India, a bachelor, he planned to marry when he returned on his next leave. He would hardly risk his chances with Lady Margaret Winston by sending home evidence of an indiscretion.

Lewis was in Italy on a European tour. They were in regular contact with Lewis; he was destined for Oxford and the Church. It could not be Lewis.

A silence ensued as there was one name left.

"Could it be...could it possibly be Cyril?" Emma asked in a very, very quiet voice.

The breakfast room was hung with doubt and possibility, hope and despair.

"No, it cannot be Cyril," her husband replied flatly and somewhat derisively.

"But, suppose he is alive?"

Cyril, the oldest son, was a captain in the British Army and had been missing, presumed dead, in the Crimea five years before.

"How could he be alive and not come home? How could he be alive and father a child in adultery? Have sense, Emma. Eat something."

"Charlotte will not like it," she admitted then, "if he is alive, and did not come home to her, and neglected her and the children all this time, and perhaps stayed in the Crimea and had a second family."

"It is a preposterous thought! Put it out of your head!"

"But he may be alive, just think! What if my Cyril is alive all this time! They never confirmed he was dead. They never found the bodies."

"He is dead, as are Corporals Brown and Enright."

Captain Cyril Leigh-Donner had led Corporals Richard Brown and James Enright up a steep hill on a scouting mission. An hour after they had left, the camp had heard shots from the hill. They had never been seen or heard of again in spite of extensive searches. They knew all three. Brown had been a young footman and Enright the coachman in the Leigh-Donner household. It had been a dreadful blow when they had heard the devastating news. The house had gone into a long mourning. The parents of the other two men lived in Spitalfields and Whitechapel, only a few miles from each other. Mrs. Leigh-Donner had visited them and given them consolation and help.

Mrs. Leigh-Donner rang the bell and ordered the child to be brought up to them. When she arrived, she was taken in her arms while she scrutinised her keenly.

"If you're looking for a resemblance, all infants look the same," her husband said, annoyed.

"She is getting past the infant stage, when resemblances begin to form. Do you not think that her eyes could look like ours, a little?"

"It's your imagination, Emma. Do not even begin to dream that Cyril is alive. This is not Cyril's child. He did not have fair hair."

She rumpled the thick fair tresses.

"Hair colour often changes!"

The child was awake and Emma, feeling restless, walked with her about the room. They came to a cabinet upon which was a group of photographs.

"Papa," sang the little one, pointing straight at a head and shoulders photo of Cyril.

"She is Cyril's! She is!" Mrs. Leigh-Donner became very excited. The colonel sighed in frustration and gulped back his coffee. If his son was alive and well somewhere, and in his wits, he was not only an adulterer, but a deserter and a disgrace. Better to believe him dead!

"It's Christmas morning, and Charlotte and the children will be here soon. Is all well with the kitchen preparations? Get your wits about you, Mrs. Leigh-Donner!" His black bushy eyebrows, the terror of his men, were drawn together in a frown.

"Yes, of course."

"Send the child down to the servants and we shall see what is to be done with her later on."

Mrs. Leigh-Donner pulled the bell again.

"Is my Cyril alive?" she asked herself, caressing her son's photograph. There must be some strange explanation for this, an explanation in which her son would come out blameless of course. He had lost his memory. That was it! He had married and regained his memory. But her ideas petered out in the improbability of it all.

∽

The housekeeper and butler said nothing downstairs about the note, and the staff were astounded at the sudden appearance of a child in their midst. She was placed in the care of the under housemaid while the servants prepared for their guests, Mrs. Cyril Leigh-Donner and her three children and their nursemaid.

They arrived at two o'clock full of Christmas merriment and gifts for their grandparents and sat down to a table laden with roast turkey stuffed with pork, baked ham dripping with syrup, golden roast potatoes, brussels sprouts, carrots, and lashings of gravy, with wine for the adults and lemonade for the children. But Charlotte noticed something wrong. Her parents-in-law were always a little sad about Cyril at Christmas, but always made the effort for the sake of the children. Today, even the jovial Grandfather was drawn and silent.

After sending the children out to play in the back garden after the Christmas pudding had been served, she asked them what the matter was. They had no choice but to inform her of the morning's happenings and to show her the note.

"It can't be Cyril," she said, her voice tremulous.

"Why not?" her mother-in-law asked sharply.

"He is dead."

"Quite so, Charlotte," Colonel Leigh-Donner said.

Charlotte's hands were shaking; she put her coffee cup back on the saucer with a giveaway tinkle. She had fallen out of love with Cyril a few years after they married, and he with her. They had been very young, she seventeen, he twenty. He had not been a bad man, but authoritarian like his father, and she had begun to suffer under his tight control and domineering way. While she never wished him dead, after seven years she would be free to remarry if he did not return. She was in love again, and Mr.

Marshall was patiently waiting until she could be declared free.

"It cannot be Cyril," she said flatly.

"She pointed to his portrait and said 'Papa,'" Mrs. Leigh-Donner said firmly. There was a very uncomfortable silence.

"What will you do with her?" Charlotte asked.

"We do not know," her father-in-law said.

"It must be a hoax," Charlotte went on. "It is well known you have a son missing, presumed dead, and someone wants a good place for their illegitimate, nobody child. Is there no way to find out for certain?"

"It appears there is not," Mrs. Leigh-Donner said. "Her clothes are not of the best quality but decent, and she is clean. She has been taken care of. She has a few words, but they are unintelligible."

After dinner, Charlotte went downstairs to the servant's hall to see the child for herself. She was sleeping on a small couch, two chairs drawn up close to it to prevent her from falling off. She gazed at her and satisfied herself that she looked nothing like Cyril's other children.

"She looks common," was her verdict. "It's a hoax, a deception, to get her a good life. She has a cunning parent who would risk that, but it is so cruel to pretend that Cyril is alive, when he is not! And why do my in-laws not think of their other two sons? It would be a good trick indeed, for either of them, to point a finger at Cyril's being alive, when they know he is not."

When her mother-in-law asked her to take the baby home with her because she had a nursery, she refused, and left that evening in a very bad temper. Unlike the first Christmas, this Christmas had been ruined by the arrival of a small child…

What will happen to this unwanted babe? How will the bairn's future unfold? Continue reading this unforgettable story in Christmas Doorstep Orphan, the new Christmas novel by Dolly Price.

Continue Reading Christmas Doorstep Orphan on Amazon

OUR GIFT TO YOU

AS A WAY TO SAY THANK YOU WE WOULD LOVE TO SEND YOU THIS BEAUTIFUL STORY FREE OF CHARGE.

Click here for your free copy of Whitechapel Waif

PureRead.com/victorian

At PureRead we publish books you can trust. Great tales without smut or swearing, but with all of the mystery and romance you expect from a great story.

Be the first to know when we release new books, take part in our fun competitions, and get surprise free books in your inbox by signing up to our free VIP Reader list.

As a welcome gift you'll receive the story of the Whitechapel Waif straight to your inbox...

Click here for your free copy of Whitechapel Waif

PureRead.com/victorian

Printed in Great Britain
by Amazon